Didi ran to the alley and flung open the heavy-lidded Dumpster. She waded through the garbage until she found the manuscript—someone had trashed it with a vengeance. Pages were ripped, stained, torn, and crumpled. A red marker had inscribed obscenities on dozens of pages.

She brought it back to the office and used cellophane tape to physically reconstruct the manuscript, but as she rearranged and taped the ripped pages, she noticed one small section that was not crumpled.

The section was a case history of a race horse brought to the Mid-Florida Equine Clinic with severe foreleg lameness stemming from radial nerve paralysis. Traditionally, the only treatment was prolonged rest, with a fifty-fifty prognosis for a cure. The case history in Eleazar Wynn's manuscript, however, claimed he'd treated the horse quickly and successfully with some very advanced laser techniques.

Didi noticed that while this section was not torn, it had received the full force of the reader's venom, including crude diagrams; particularly, small circles and crosses.

It was the groups of circles—usually three together, sometimes touching—that riveted her attention. She began to feel a profound uneasiness. . . .

Dr. Nightingale
Seeks
Greener Pastures

A DEIRDRE QUINN
NIGHTINGALE MYSTERY

Lydia Adamson

A SIGNET BOOK

SIGNET
Published by New American Library, a division of
Penguin Putnam Inc., 375 Hudson Street,
New York, New York 10014, U.S.A.
Penguin Books Ltd, 27 Wrights Lane,
London W8 5TZ, England
Penguin Books Australia Ltd,
Ringwood, Victoria, Australia
Penguin Books Canada Ltd, 10 Alcorn Avenue,
Toronto, Ontario, Canada M4V 3B2
Penguin Books (N.Z.) Ltd, 182–190 Wairau Road,
Auckland 10, New Zealand

Penguin Books Ltd, Registered Offices:
Harmondsworth, Middlesex, England

First published by Signet, an imprint of New American Library,
a division of Penguin Putnam Inc.

First Printing, July 2000
10 9 8 7 6 5 4 3 2 1

PUBLISHER'S NOTE
This is a work of fiction. Names, characters, places, and incidents are
either the product of the author's imagination or are used fictitiously, and
any resemblance to actual persons, living or dead, business establishments,
events, or locales is entirely coincidental.

Chapter 1

Deirdre Quinn Nightingale, D.V.M., sat primly on a bench in Philadelphia's 30th Street Station.

She had left Hillsbrook at eight in the morning, boarded a train to Penn Station in Poughkeepsie, changed for the train to Philadelphia, and was now waiting for a connection to Atlantic City.

It was just past noon, on an unseasonably warm March day.

Young Dr. Nightingale was dressed in purposefully severe fashion—charcoal gray business suit with a longish skirt—because she was headed for the Eastern States Veterinary Convention and it was important that she look her age . . . almost thirty.

It was a bitter fact of life for her that sometimes she was still carded when ordering a drink in places where she was not known. She was pretty and exceptionally slight, with short-cut dark hair. These facts of her existence always made for age confusion, particularly when she was working in the field and attired in her usual outfit: well-worn overalls or jeans. In short, Dr. Nightingale sometimes looked like a little girl.

This was the first professional meeting she had attended in almost four years, and only the third since she had left veterinary school. But she was not treating the trip as a getaway—a much-deserved vacation. No, her reason for attending this conference was an altogether practical one.

Dr. Nightingale, in a hard-nosed look at the facts, had acknowledged that her veterinary practice was failing.

There were simply too few dairy farms remaining in Dutchess County. The cows had abandoned her.

She realized she had only two options if she wanted to go on in her profession, keep her house, her property and her animals, and provide a roof over the heads of the four "elves," a motley collection of household retainers that she had inherited from her late mother.

Option number one: Expand the small-animal practice—dogs, parakeets, kittens, and so on.

Option number two: Hook up with one of the

big new breeding stables in the area, the ones that raised Thoroughbred horses.

The first option was the more intelligent, of course, but Didi simply had no interest in being a small-animal vet.

The second choice intrigued her. Horses had long been a passion of hers. She went for this option. The trouble was, her experience in the field was meager (especially with racehorses) even if her talents were great. And she was simply not up-to-date in equine medicine.

She needed to master the hottest new vocabulary of equine diagnosis and treatment. That was why she was waiting for the train to take her to the convention at Atlantic City, where, presumably, she would find out what was new and make some valuable contacts for getting work in this area.

Actually, during the four-day convention, Didi would be sleeping thirty miles south of Atlantic City in the small seaside resort town of Cape May. The convention committee had reasoned, correctly, that many veterinarians probably didn't care for casinos and casino culture. So alternate accommodations were being offered—in Cape May, which was noted for its attractiveness to watercolorists, antiquers, and birdwatchers. Dr. Nightingale was not really interested in any of those activities, but she certainly found them all more appealing than gambling.

The convention—with its many exhibits by pharmaceutical companies, electronic imaging corporations, and pet food conglomerates; with its lectures and scholarly meetings—was to be conducted at the brand-new Atlantic City convention center on the boardwalk.

The loudspeaker in the 30th Street Station announced the boarding of New Jersey Transit train number 806 bound for Atlantic City—gate number 5.

Didi picked up her leather attaché case and her aged valise with the leather straps around it, and headed for the gate.

By one-thirty she was registering at the convention center. She received her ID badge, the thick convention program, and confirmation of her bed-and-breakfast reservation in Cape May.

By two o'clock she was on the minibus, heading south. By two-thirty she was ensconced in her room, which was quite charming. It had a shower, but the bathroom was down the hall. The inn was a lovely old frame house with a wooden swing on its porch. It was only two blocks from the ocean, and she could hear and smell the breakers from her open window.

After unpacking, Didi sat on the bed and carefully went through the convention program, checking off meetings, seminars, and lectures she wished to attend.

The first "must" lecture was scheduled for late the next morning. The speaker would be Eleazar Wynn, a very successful racing vet. Didi had heard him speak in her last year of vet school. He was an impressive man. Tomorrow's topic would be "Lameness in the Rear Leg: New Problems, New Procedures."

Oh yes, that was definitely a must.

There was a knock at the door. Didi looked up, a bit startled. Was someone calling on her so soon after her arrival? She didn't know a soul in the area. Another knock. She walked over to the door and opened it.

"Hello! I'm your neighbor, Ann Huggins. Are you here for the EVA convention?"

"Yes."

"Good! So am I!"

The young woman in the doorway had an explosive, staccato way of speaking. In addition, she was, frankly, strange-looking: at least six feet tall, stooped, with stringy yellow hair and very bright green eyes over which were smeared bold patches of eye shadow. She was dressed in denim from head to toe. For some reason, she reminded Didi of the old R&B song "Mustang Sally."

"I hope you won't consider me a pest, but could you do me a favor?" the big blonde said. "A big favor! I mean . . . well, where the hell is the town of Cape May?"

Didi was startled by the question, perplexed. "You are *in* the town of Cape May," she replied. "You're standing in that town now." Then, she suddenly understood the meaning of Ann Huggins's question. "Are you talking about stores and such—shopping?"

"Yes! Yes, exactly. Stores."

"If you give me five minutes, I'll show you," Didi said, then added, "My name is Deirdre Quinn Nightingale, by the way."

"Ha! What a mouthful that is! What do people call you?"

"Didi, mostly. A few people just call me Nightingale."

"I like Nightingale. I'll call you that. You in private practice?"

"Yes. I work in Hillsbrook. That's Dutchess County, New York."

"Well, *again*, we're neighbors—almost. I'm from Toronto. You get ready; I'll be downstairs waiting." And with that she was gone.

Didi wondered how—why—anyone could consider Toronto to be "almost" the neighbor to

Dutchess County. This tall woman with the piercing voice *was* a bit strange.

She closed the door, finished looking through the convention brochures, then went downstairs.

"I was here in Cape May once before, a few years ago," Didi explained as she led Ann Huggins away from the inn. "If I recall, the main shopping area is only three blocks from the ocean, but you have to reach it circuitously."

"That doesn't make sense."

"I know it doesn't seem to, but it's true. You have to follow the contours of the hills, not the streets. This town is essentially built on dunes." Didi stopped there, realizing that instead of clearing up the confusion, she was causing more. Within five minutes she had navigated them into the center of town—actually a village mall consisting of several fetching cobblestone blocks where vehicular access was severely restricted. There were restaurants and shops of all kinds, many street vendors and performers, and plenty of benches to rest on.

"At this moment, Dr. Nightingale," Ann Huggins announced, "I have two powerful desires. A grilled cheese and bacon sandwich is the first, and a new pair of running shoes is the second. Will you allow me to treat you to one of the former as thanks for your yeoman directional help?"

"Sure," Didi agreed. "I'm hungry."

They each had an absolutely delicious grilled sandwich in a hamburger place called the Broasted Bun. During the repast, Mustang Sally revealed that she was a partner in a successful dog and cat clinic in Toronto and was really at the convention only to "play."

"Does that shock you?" She eyed Didi teasingly.

"No. In fact, I find it laudable. Unfortunately, right now I have other fish to fry."

"Well, you go and fry them good," Ann counseled. She finished her sandwich and compulsively cleared the table of crumbs, all the while expanding on what her Toronto establishment provided for clients and patients: surgery, kennels, grooming, testing, adoption services, inpatient and outpatient services, a retail shop for pet supplies, dietary supplements, and so on. Didi was properly impressed. Then Ann Huggins ordered coffee and apple crumb pie.

"You may find this difficult to believe, Nightingale, but I find male veterinarians sexy."

Didi hardly knew how to respond. All she could think to say was, "I was head over heels for one once."

"What happened?"

"He dumped me."

"Oh. Well, I never said they were nice . . . or bright. Only that I find them sexy. I don't know— they have a goofy mixture of innocence and venality. You know what I'm saying?"

"Sort of," Didi replied, but she really didn't.

When they exited the restaurant, daylight was beginning to fade, the wind was up, and there was a hint of rain. More than a hint, actually. Several sea-laden drops landed on them.

"I am going to get those running shoes or die!" Ann Huggins exclaimed. "But I've imposed upon you long enough. Please feel free to abandon me in my hour of need. Without remorse."

Didi laughed. She was beginning to like Ann Huggins.

"No," she said. "I'll take a look with you."

They found a perfect source two blocks away. The small store was chock-full of athletic shoes and gear but seemed a bit quirky. The window display featured nothing but bedroom slippers.

"I definitely do not want one of those chain stores," Ann remarked.

"Then here you are. This place seems to be very nonchain," Didi answered, realizing even as she said it that this strange young vet had a way of eliciting irrational comments from her.

The store was long and narrow. On one side, up and down the wall, sneakers and running shoes of all shapes, colors, and functions were displayed.

Along the opposite wall was a long row of benches where customers might sit and try on their prospective purchases. Between the benches were freestanding mirrors in which they could evaluate and admire themselves in their selections.

In the center—more or less dividing the deep room—were artfully piled boxes; it took Didi a few minutes to realize that this was not just a decorative display but the store's actual merchandise—the stock. There was something rather chic about the arrangement.

"Look at these!" Ann exclaimed in wonder, picking up one shoe.

It was a woman's running shoe, on sale for $107.95, regularly priced at $124.95.

The uppers were purple; the lowers were gray; and the bottoms were white. The shoe's leather ties were intricately laced.

Ann Huggins kept examining the shoe, turning it this way and that in wonder. "Actually I don't run," she confessed.

Didi noticed the salespeople for the first time. One man was seated on the bench at the back of the store reading a newspaper. Another man, a young Asian, was fiddling with one of the boxes in the center aisle. He was watching Ann and Didi surreptitiously, as if trying to decide whether they were serious customers.

Didi looked toward the front of the store, where a customer was seated on one of the benches, staring down at an array of shoes on the floor. Obviously the poor man was having trouble making a decision.

Didi continued to look at him. She knew the man, she realized. But from where? From Hillsbrook? No, that wasn't it.

Of course! It came to her. That was Eleazar Wynn—the vet whose lecture she planned to attend. She had seen him only once before—years ago—but she remembered his distinctive, craggy face. There was no doubt about it; that was Wynn.

She turned back to Ann Huggins, intending to point out the famous vet to her, but Ann had moved deeper into the store, lured by the rack of shoes at the back.

Didi caught up with her.

"I've lost focus," Ann complained. "I've forgotten what the hell I was looking for in the first place."

"Running shoes," offered Didi.

"Yes! Yes, you're right. Thanks."

The salesman who had been so engrossed in

the newspaper suddenly leaped out of his seat, the paper falling to the floor.

The young Asian man was now shouting wildly.

Both men began to run toward the front of the shop.

Didi and Ann looked at each other in confusion.

Ann was looking around frantically. "What is it? . . . What? . . . *What!*"

Didi took off after the two running men, pulling Ann with her.

The four of them formed a circle around the customer. Eleazar Wynn slouched in his chair—dead. A long, pencil-thin black object stuck out of the main artery of his neck. He had died within seconds of being stabbed, without uttering a sound.

The sneakers he had been inspecting were now awash in blood. Bright red arterial blood. His.

Chapter 2

Dr. Nightingale was the last one to be interrogated in the east wing of the Cape May Town Hall—the administration site of the Cape May Police Department.

The interrogation commenced about 9 P.M., some four hours after the murder.

She did not like the New Jersey State Trooper homicide detective who interrogated her—Craig Nova. The feeling seemed to be mutual.

She was seated in front of an old-fashioned, very long wood table. Detective Nova circled the table as he questioned her. He was a short, blond, heavily muscled individual with hair that started very low down on his brow.

"You seem to be the only witness in the store who knew the victim's identity," he noted.

"Is that why I'm still here?" Didi responded bitterly. Nova didn't reply. He waited.

Didi continued: "Yes. I know exactly who he was. He was one of the reasons I came to this convention. He was a very famous horse doctor."

"Then why didn't you say hello to him?"

"I didn't know him personally. I knew of him. Besides, I was with a friend."

"You mean Ann Huggins."

"Yes."

"A friend? But I thought you two had just met. Isn't that true?"

"Yes."

"Did Miss Huggins know who he was?"

"I don't know."

"You didn't mention to Ann that the famous Dr. Eleazar Wynn was in the store?"

"No, I didn't."

"Why not?"

"I was going to . . . but something interceded."

"What?"

"I don't know. I don't remember. Maybe she found a pair of running shoes that she liked."

"Don't you find it strange, Dr. Nightingale, that five individuals are in a shoe store . . . one is stabbed in the neck by a sharp object . . . bleeds to death . . . and not one of the other four individuals is aware of what is happening? Until, of course, the man is dead."

"Yes. I find that strange. I find my own lack of awareness strange."

"What type of veterinarian are you?"

"Large animal, mostly. Dairy cows and the like."

"Horses also?"

"Of course."

Detective Nova finally sat down, directly across from her. Dr. Nightingale folded her hands on the table. She had no idea why she had taken such an instant dislike to this man. His questions were reasonable; his demeanor polite.

Maybe it was his hooded eyes. Yes. That was it. Hooded. Goats were like that sometimes. One had to be careful around them. One was often surprised. One was often made to look foolish in front of a client. And sometimes, one could get hurt.

She stared at the thumbs of her folded hands and suddenly smiled. Any image of goats always brought back her most satisfying veterinary memory.

She had been back home in Hillsbrook for only a month or two and was starting out on her veterinary career. "Something very strange is happening to my goats," the distraught caller had said.

Didi and her new assistant, Charlie Gravis, had rushed over to the man's farm.

They found a herd of twenty or so French

15

Alpines. Beautiful milk goats they were, with erect ears, long heads, and straight or slightly dished noses. They presented themselves in a wide variety of colors—brown and white, black and white, solids.

Yes, they were acting strange. They were slamming their heads into one other.

Fresh out of vet school, she initiated a by-the-book, hands-on medical examination supplemented by a vigorous interrogation of the goatherder, centering on one particularly aggressive, head-slamming goat called Lucinda.

Was Lucinda alert and inquisitive? Was her appetite constant? Was she chewing her cud? Were her eyes bright and without discharge? Was her nose dry and cool? Was her coat clean and glossy? Any abscesses under her jaw? On the legs? Were her droppings firm and pelleted? Urine light and brown? Without traces of blood? Was her breathing regular? Gait steady? Favoring any one of her feet? Changes in quantity or quality of milk yield? Any stringiness in her milk? Any undue sensitivity in her udders?

Armed with the answers, she confidently diagnosed: *CCN*. Cerebral cortico necrosis, a disorder based on thiamine deficiency.

Then she realized she was wrong, and corrected the diagnosis: "circling disease," or listeriosis.

But she soon realized she was wrong there, also.

And then she had the brilliant intuition that the reason Lucinda might be slamming her head was that she had an itch in her ear. So she swabbed out the goat's right ear, discovered mites, and realized Lucinda and her companions had a dose of a mild and curable mange.

Oh, what a joy that day had been!

Sitting there, years later, as part of a murder investigation, the good memories of that time and place were almost intoxicating.

"What else can you tell me about Eleazar Wynn, other than that he was a famous horse doctor?"

Detective Nova's question broke her reverie.

"Nothing."

"Surely you must know something."

"Like what?"

"I mean—was there any whiff of scandal or trouble about the man? Were there any rumors about him? Thief? Adulterer? Pederast? Fetishist? Plagiarist? Compulsive gambler? Drunk? Murderer?"

Didi burst out laughing. It was the wrong response, but she couldn't help herself. Nova's "hoodedness" increased. This fool, she thought, looks like he's about to hiss, like a snake rather than a goat.

"I definitely heard rumors that he was an impaler," Didi finally quipped. Detective Nova did not appreciate the joke. Didi felt stupid for trying to be funny. But she was tired now; very, very tired. The day was over. The man was dead, but the convention had barely begun. There were still four days left, with or without Dr. Wynn. And in a hundred barns on a hundred racetracks from one ocean to the other, at least one horse was pulling up lame.

The "elves" were assembled in the kitchen of the large old Nightingale home in Hillsbrook, Dutchess County, New York.

It was late, almost midnight, and way past their bedtime. They were all worried, in their fashion. The boss hadn't called from Jersey as she had promised.

Trent Tucker, the young handyman, was fast asleep at the table, his head in his arms.

Abigail Little, just a year older than Trent, was standing next to the table, silent as usual, but alert, expertly braiding her long yellow hair. Abigail took care of the yard dogs, the pigs, and Dr. Nightingales's Thoroughbred horse—Promise Me.

Mrs. Tunney, the head elf, was moaning about the problem. "Miss Quinn is in trouble. Miss Quinn is in trouble."

When discussing Dr. Nightingale with the other elves, Mrs. Tunney always called her Miss Quinn, Quinn being the maiden name of Didi's mother.

Charlie Gravis, Didi's geriatric veterinary assistant, was trying to calm the old lady.

"New Jersey is a whole different world," he noted.

"They have phones there, don't they? They have phones in hotels. She's supposed to be in a hotel, or a motel," Mrs. Tunney affirmed, with anguish.

Abigail walked to the stove and brought back the coffee pot, refilling cups. Charlie kicked the bottom of the table, waking Trent Tucker.

The phone in the small-animal office down the hall began to ring.

"It can't be her," Charlie noted. "She would call on the house phone." He pointed to the extension on the kitchen wall as if the others were dim-witted.

The phone stopped after—just after—the fourth ring, a split second before the answering machine would have kicked in.

Thirty seconds later it started to ring again.

Mrs. Tunney ordered Trent: "You go pick that up." He jumped up from the table and vanished down the hall.

"I knew something bad was going to happen," she whispered to Charlie.

"We don't know yet if anything at all has happened, much less something bad," Charlie Gravis cautioned.

"I knew it the moment I saw that Voegler fella back in Hillsbrook," Mrs. Tunney explained.

Charlie made a face but didn't answer. It was futile to try to combat Mrs. Tunney's irrational hatred of Allie Voegler, the Hillsbrook cop who had been reinstated after a rather lengthy suspension for smacking around a witness in a trooper barracks on Route 44. Charlie knew his boss had dumped Voegler. They weren't lovers anymore, they weren't engaged anymore, and they probably weren't even friends.

Mrs. Tunney knew these facts also, but she just couldn't absorb them.

According to Mrs. Tunney, all the money problems currently afflicting Dr. Deirdre Quinn Nightingale stemmed from man problems. And that meant Voegler. She hated his first name— Allie. She hated the way he dressed—flannel shirts. She hated the way he lounged, talked, even the way he looked at people. He was, Mrs.

Tunney believed—and this was a word she used very rarely—crude.

Trent Tucker stepped back into the kitchen.

"Yeah. It was her. She says she's sorry she called so late. She says she was in a shoe store, and there was some kind of emergency. She's OK. No problem. She'll call tomorrow about six. Six in the evening."

"That's it? *That's all?*" Mrs. Tunney screamed at him.

Trent Tucker shrugged. He said nothing. Mrs. Tunney was a freight train now. She could not be stopped.

"What kind of emergency? Was she hurt? Did she call from the hospital? Did you get the number?"

Trent Tucker finally threw up his hands. "No, no, you got it all wrong. She's fine. No hospital. No problem."

Okay, Charlie Gravis thought, it definitely is time to intercede.

"Did she say anything about the checkbook?" Charlie asked.

It was strictly a ploy . . . a diversion . . . a meaningless question . . . a detour . . . a mask. It worked.

Mrs. Tunney turned her wrath on him. "What are you up to, Charlie? Miss Quinn didn't mention no checkbook when she left. Are you hiding something from me?"

Trent Tucker was quick to take advantage of the diversion. He slipped quietly out of the room. Abigail began to clear the cups from the table.

"I'm confused. What did I say? Checkbook? No, no. I meant appointment book. You know, the one we keep in the office. The one she usually carries in her Jeep."

Mrs. Tunney declared loudly: "The Jeep is here! She's there!"

From the night outside the kitchen windows suddenly came a strange series of sounds—yapping, howling, groaning. They came from the north, from the stand of pines behind the house. A sure sign of spring. Feral dogs in a pack in the woods. Starting to run deer. Yes, it was a definite sign of spring in still heavily wooded Hillsbrook.

Fatigue suddenly grabbed Mrs. Tunney by the throat. "Good night," she whispered and headed toward her room.

Then Abigail left and Charlie Gravis was alone.

He would, he realized, be the last to get to sleep, when he should have been the first. After all, he was the oldest and the most valuable of the elves. Yes, he was by far the most valuable. Everyone freely admitted that it was Charlie

Gravis's cow sense that had turned Nightingale into the accomplished practitioner she now was.

Everyone in Hillsbrook knew that old dairy farmers are worth their weight in gold. They have the power . . . the X-ray eyes.

Sitting there in the kitchen, listening to the feral dogs, he suddenly recalled a radio program from his youth—"Captain Midnight and the Secret Squadron."

Why that popped into his head at that moment, he hadn't the slightest idea.

"I should have known you were a hopeless romantic," Ann Huggins whispered.

She and Didi were seated in the lovely small lecture hall, attending a dead man's lecture. The stand-in, a veterinarian from California, had read a short memorial speech at the outset and then launched into his own ruminations on the abnormal rear leg of the racehorse.

"You mean because I'm attending the lecture?"

"Yes. And because you dragged me here with you, Nightingale."

"But I didn't drag you, Ann. I just made the suggestion. Anyway . . . how does coming here make me a romantic?"

"Because the man you wanted to hear turned up dead. Yet you believe absolutely that his replacement will also tell you things you want to hear. Some people would call that optimism. Me, I call it romanticism."

"Maybe I came here out of respect for the memory of Eleazar Wynn. Maybe all the people here feel that way," Didi explained. Her new friend, she realized, could be a pain in the neck.

They listened together in silence. The lecturer was not cutting-edge. He was basically just presenting a short list of abnormalities of the rear leg and related problems—dislocation of the sacroiliac joint, bursitis, stifle lameness, bog spavin, capped hock, and the like.

When he reached "upward fixation of the patella," Ann Huggins groaned, leaned over, and whispered again: "No more for me, Nightingale. I'm walking out of here right now, turning right on the boardwalk, and going into the first casino I see. Pick me up when this is over. I'll be at the slot machines."

She walked out. Didi sank down in her plush seat. This woman, Ann Huggins, had fastened on her. That kind of thing was, of course, an occupational hazard of attending conventions.

Eleazar Wynn being murdered wasn't.

Still, the mess had receded quickly. Not the loss, no, but the mess itself. She had now, less than a day after the murder, only a very fuzzy memory of the shoe store; of running toward the front of the store; of that strange scene of bone-white pallor and bloody stains.

As if a thirsty vampire had stuck a drinking straw into the man's neck.

Oh, everything was a blur now. Except the loss. If there was such a thing as "the horse world," it would surely miss that man.

Didi closed her eyes. What was the object sticking out of the good vet's neck? She didn't know. It wasn't a straw.

Not a knife, either.

Maybe some kind of weird darning needle.

Maybe a letter opener.

The lecturer began to discourse on the vertebral column.

Didi forgot the dead man and remembered a dead horse, at least two years dead. The horse was afflicted with tetanus. There were back spasms. Muscle spasms. Then a fracture of the back near the twelfth thoracic vertebra. Didi had put the horse down.

The lecturer droned on. Abnormalities of the equine rear leg, Didi knew, were as extensive and as diverse as abnormalities of the human heart— and twice as mysterious.

I'm hungry, she thought. Not just hungry. Starving. She realized why. She hadn't eaten since the previous day, with Ann, before they had gone into that shoe store. No dinner last night. No breakfast this morning.

She walked out of the lecture hall to hunt up Ann Huggins.

Charlie Gravis and his friend Ike Badian were sipping steins of exotic ale in the new Hillsbrook Pub on Main Street.

It was two o'clock in the afternoon.

"We're like country gentlemen," Ike noted, his bitterness almost but not quite submerged.

Charlie reached over and patted his friend on the shoulder.

"Hell," he said, "I think you're taking it pretty good, Ike. When I had to shut my barn operation down, people took my shotgun away."

Ike grinned. He was bitter—but not suicidal. He was two years older than Charlie, and that was old indeed. He had lasted longer than anyone. And now he was out. Only four cows left. The machinery dead. The back too old to bend and milk. The head, heart, and hand no longer in it . . . no longer capable. Over. Gone. Out.

"I have no sympathy for myself," Ike declared, playing the hero a bit.

"So now what?" Charlie queried.

"Maybe your girl vet needs another assistant."

"She doesn't even have enough work for herself."

"Well, there's always the poorhouse."

"You have social security, Ike?"

"No. You?"

"Of course not. You know old dairy farmers never paid in. Hell, I never filed a real tax return . . . never made enough. I thought maybe you did things a little different."

"But, Charlie, you had a much bigger operation than me."

"Bigger ain't better."

Ike ordered two whiskeys.

The bartender poured two shots of Fleishmann's rye whiskey into elegant shot glasses. He picked up Ike's ten-dollar bill from the top of the bar, rang the drinks up, and came back with a single dollar bill, which he laid delicately in front of Ike. Then he meandered off.

"Do you see what I see?" Ike asked Charlie.

"Rye whiskey?"

"No. The buck."

"OK. I see the buck."

"That means this character charged me four-fifty for a lousy shot of rye. Is he insane?"

"Calm down, Ike. In places like this it's the going rate."

"Places like this? What the hell are you talking about, Charlie? This is Hillsbrook! This is dairy cow country!"

Charlie realized a crisis was afoot. Ike was losing control. There was nothing so pathetic and dangerous as a drooling, bumbling, bankrupt old cow man who drank in the afternoon and thought he'd been cheated.

Charlie picked up the shot glass and swallowed the contents.

He choked a bit as the whiskey went down, then recovered and said: "Drink up, Ike. I need some help."

"For what?" Ike asked, distracted but still glaring at the bartender.

"Gotta do an errand for the boss. Gotta see a man about a horse," Charlie said. He figured he would make up something a little more real once he got Ike safely out of the pub.

Sure enough, old Ike bought it hook, line, and sinker. They marched out of the pub like two brothers about to enlist in the French Foreign Legion.

Chapter 3

Dr. Deirdre Quinn Nightingale arrived back in Hillsbrook three days after she had left for the convention.

She came back a day earlier than she had planned, having made no lucrative contacts.

At 6 A.M. the next morning she resumed her usual yogic breathing exercise in the backyard, seated in the lotus position.

She always did her exercises at this hour, or even earlier, and always outside. The more inclement the weather, the better. She didn't do yoga for health. She did it for discipline, to develop a kind of stoicism, and to think more clearly. And she followed only one particular yogic regimen—based on breathing in and out at various speeds and various degrees of blockage.

Of course, once in a while, when times were

very tense or troubled, she would do the exercises anywhere and anytime.

She had learned this form of yoga from a girl who had briefly shared an apartment with her in Philadelphia while both were attending vet school.

The roommate's name was Olive. She came from a wealthy California family and her passions were shoplifting, esoteric forms of yoga, and old Clint Eastwood spaghetti westerns, in that order.

When Didi had traveled to India and Southeast Asia after vet school, the impetus being a broken heart—she had been seduced and abandoned by the only man she had ever loved wildly—she had persisted in doing the yoga, thinking she would be able to get pointers from the natives. After all, yoga, in all its forms, was Indian.

She was there, technically, on a grant to study the health problems of Asian elephants being utilized as work animals. This meant she spent most of her time in remote jungle logging camps—where the elephants were located.

Most of the people who lived and worked in the camps knew virtually nothing about yoga. And when they saw her doing the breathing exercises . . . when they saw her close one nostril and then the other and breathe so slowly it appeared that she was dying . . . when they saw her breathe so fast she appeared to be hyperventilating . . . when they saw all this, they thought she was quite mad.

That was India, then.

This was Hillsbrook, now.

The morning was dark, cold, and rainy. Didi was quite happy. Let it rain. Let the wind howl. She was happy to be home. She was happy to be going on rounds again.

When the breathing exercises were completed, she walked into the house and through the kitchen, where the elves were assembled for Mrs. Tunney's obligatory oatmeal. As usual, Didi took a cup of coffee from the communal pot and carried it upstairs to her room.

At seven-thirty she left the house and climbed into the red Jeep. She started the engine and idled it. Then Charlie Gravis climbed in and off they went.

"First stop?" he inquired.

"The pig man," Didi replied.

The rain had stopped, but the morning sun was obstructed by a long wedge of clouds.

Halfway to the pig man's spread, Dr. Nightingale spotted Albert Voegler's unmarked police cruiser in the rearview mirror. Charlie picked up on it a few seconds later. "True love," he speculated. She grinned and pulled off the road, onto the shoulder.

The vehicle following the Jeep passed it, executed a daring U-turn, and pulled up beside the Jeep so that the driver-side windows of the two vehicles were parallel.

Didi and Allie rolled their windows down simultaneously—a pas de deux of ex-lovers. They had spoken twice since Voegler had returned to town. Brief, uncomfortable, perplexing conversations. To wit . . . whatever had been was over.

"Where you been?" he asked.

"Away."

"Yeah, I knew that. Away where?"

"Argentina."

"OK. Look, I just thought it would make sense, Didi, if we had a calm, quiet dinner together. You know what I'm saying? Everything between us seems to have just fallen apart. Very fast."

She felt a sudden stab of longing. She didn't know for what. Perhaps, she thought, she wanted to console him. After all, the man had been through a lot . . . what with the suspension and the mandated psychiatric treatment.

Their eyes were dancing all over each other's faces but not meeting directly.

Like two deranged moths over a candle, Charlie thought. He said not a word.

"It's a bad time right now, Allie. Give me a few weeks."

"Sure. I got nothing but time. You on call now?"

"Yes."

"Who?"

"The pig man."

Albert Voegler threw back his head and laughed: "Is that idiot still in Hillsbrook?"

"Yes," Dr. Nightingale said, closing her window suddenly. Voegler followed suit and backed his vehicle off the shoulder so that the Jeep could return to the road.

Five minutes later, the young vet and Gravis drove through the stone markers of Luis Ragobert's farm.

Everyone in Hillsbrook thought Ragobert was crazy. Except Didi. She thought he was a pathetic visionary who would have been quite acceptable in a nineteenth-century novel.

Ragobert had decided to take on the entire hog husbandry establishment, which believed—and had believed for a long time—that pigs should be fed a balanced scientific diet, preferably in dry pellet form.

Ragobert was violently opposed to this cornerstone of pig farming. He was convinced that pigs should eat random slop—human leftovers, whether animal, vegetable, or mineral.

So he had come to Hillsbrook and set up his own scientific station. He kept six breeds of pigs: Berkshire, Hampshire, Yorkshire, Duroc, Chester White, and Poland China. For each breed he maintained two separate families. One was fed exclusively scientific pellet feed. The other was fed slop from the Ragobert household.

For ten years he had been trying to prove that slop-fed pigs were healthier and converted more of what they ate into meat.

No one had ever printed his findings. Didi had no idea what the findings actually were. Ragobert paid her to visit his place twice a month and merely walk through the pens. She never examined a single pig. All she had to do was make the walk . . . a kind of unofficial official inspection, as if by having a qualified vet on the premises awarded the establishment with authenticity. After the ridiculous inspection, Ragobert would usually ask her a question or two about esoteric porcine disorders that Didi had never come across in her practice. This was done over coffee and cake that Ragobert prepared.

No one knew where he'd come from. South America? Iceland? Or where his money had come from. Industry? Drug running? He rarely spoke to anyone. He rarely went into town. His solitude seemed to suit him.

Of course, the village of Hillsbrook was used to eccentric wealthy gentleman farmers. At one point they had become a plague on the landscape, many of their projects much more bizarre and obscure than Mr. Ragobert's.

The so-called pig man was waiting for them in front of the magnificent stone barn. He was dressed, as usual, in a white butcher's smock, high boots, and a woolen cap. Why he wore such an outfit was unclear—no hog was ever butchered on his property. He was a tall man, heavyset running to fat, with a pronounced slouch.

As usual, he was painstakingly formal.

"How good to see you again, Dr. Nightingale. And you, too, Mr. Gravis."

He led them into the barn. Didi marched from one pen to another. At each pen, Ragobert went into his spiel, identifying the breed as if Didi had never seen it before, and identifying which group within each breed category was on which diet. Didi and her assistant tried to look interested, earnest, even though they could recite the spiel by heart if called upon.

Charlie kept quiet. He was watching carefully . . . his eyes were open. Charlie was now and had always been fascinated by pigs.

He kept pigs himself; raised them, sold them, and slaughtered them.

And in his fashion, he loved them.

Yes, Charlie Gravis loved pigs, but not the way Ragobert did, and surely not the way Didi loved them.

His was a strange, subtle, old-man's love. A secret love. He never spoke about it, because people wouldn't understand.

Pigs were pigs. And people were people.

Mainly—most of all—it was the nose of the pig that anchored Charlie's awe and respect.

The pig's snout is one of the most wondrous creations in the world. It functions as the eyes, ears, and computer of the porcine identity. He uses it for love and hate. He keeps it tender and moist, like the tip of an elephant's trunk, which is the only object in the world that resembles it.

What the pig knows, he knows through his nose.

Funny, Charlie thought as he followed Nightingale following Ragobert from pen to pen, he'd been a dairy farmer all his life, but he'd never met a cow he loved as much as his Spotted Poland China sow, Sara.

From the barn, which was meticulously clean,

Luis Ragobert marched them into the kitchen of his large sprawling house for fresh coffee and hot, homemade corn muffins with butter and quince jam.

After the repast Luis questioned Didi about a recent epidemic of swine flu on the island of Formosa. Didi knew precious little, but told him what she had gleaned from her professional reading. Soon the visit was over.

As they drove off the property, Charlie noted: "I know the guy's crazy, but when I'm around him, he seems completely rational."

Didi grimaced.

"You keep pigs, Charlie. You know them. Do you agree with his theories?"

"Damn right I do, Doc. Give them slop. Hell, if I was a pig, I'd rather eat corn cobs, dumped oatmeal, and steak gristle than the most highfalutin nutritious crap those chemists could dream up."

Didi hesitated before replying.

She was about to tell Charlie that the pig stores thirty-five percent of all he consumes no matter what he consumes. And that the pig is one of the few animals that never overeats no matter how much food is available.

But to give Charlie this intellectual fodder went against her grain. It could be used to confirm Ragobert's thesis. Deep down, she knew, old Charlie hated vets, veterinary science, and the scientific theories of livestock nutrition. Like Ragobert, he was a Luddite. He could be dangerous.

So all she did say, a few minutes later, was, "He always pays his bills."

"Amen," Charlie replied.

Rose Vigdor left the health food store on Main Street in Hillsbrook with two large bags of assorted chips—the food on which she essentially existed along with many exotic juices, pulped.

She headed toward her battered old Volvo, which contained three yapping dogs playing tag over what was left of the upholstery.

Twenty yards before she reached her car, she was astonished to see Albert Voegler in front of the Hillsbrook Pub. He was just standing there, lounging, smoking a cigarette. She rarely ran into him on the street.

She nodded as she passed.

He called out: "How are your dogs?"

This was stranger still—this attempt to be civil, almost friendly, almost genuinely concerned. She was so struck by his behavior that she stopped in her tracks and stared at him.

After all, Voegler knew she was Didi's closest

friend in Hillsbrook, and he didn't like any of her friends. He believed, with some reason, that they badmouthed him to Didi. In addition, Allie didn't like her personally. She was perfectly aware that he thought she was a goofy dilettante—a city girl who had come to the country to play Thoreau, eat organic avocado chips, and live in a half-renovated, half-furnished, unheated barn.

He repeated the question, treating her as if she were deaf: "How are your dogs?"

"Fine," she replied, smiling. "And how are yours?"

"I don't have any dogs. Or cats."

"A man needs companionship," she said blithely, and then instantly regretted the unintended cruelty of her words. He flinched. His face set ominously. She knew Didi and he were history and it pained him a whole lot more than it pained her friend.

"Can I buy you a drink?" he asked suddenly.

Now what is going on here? she asked herself. Does he want to cry on someone's shoulder? Someone who knows Didi? Someone who could function as a messenger to her?

Fat chance.

Or maybe, possibly, he was going to make a play for her. Was he that stupid? Anything was possible when one was dealing with a man with a broken heart. Especially a rural cop with a gun.

Impassive again, he waited for an answer, his signature flannel shirt open at the collar and flared out over his pants. The only plainclothes officer on the eight-man Hillsbrook Police Department, Albert Voegler was big and brawny, with a wild shock of hair. He had shaved off his beard and now looked much younger than his thirty-two years. People were a bit afraid of him, not because of his size but because of his unpredictability. He always seemed on the verge of exploding into action.

In the end she refused the invitation. "It's a bit early in the day for me. Maybe some other time."

Voegler nodded and started walking away, flinging his cigarette into the gutter.

"Hold on," she called.

He turned. Rose didn't know exactly what had just happened between them, but she had the feeling that she had behaved badly, unkindly. She had to salvage the moment somehow. She reached into her bag and pulled out a package of chips.

"Want some?" she asked.

"You must be kidding."

Suddenly angry and embarrassed—both by

her offer and by his response—Rose turned on her heel and walked quickly to her car.

It was eleven-twenty in the evening. Didi had fallen fast asleep in her mother's rocking chair, fully clothed, while reading an old book from her mother's shelf—W. H. Hudson's essays on gauchos and wildlife on the pampas of Argentina.

The writing was so lovely, so archaic, that it had put her out quickly . . . simply lulled her into sleep with visions of the high grass on the vast fertile plains of an exotic land.

"Miss Quinn! Miss Quinn! There's a man at the door!"

Mrs. Tunney's words crackled through the door and startled her awake.

As the chief elf and Didi walked down the stairs together, Mrs. Tunney kept saying, "He won't give his name. All he'll say is he needs to talk to you."

Usually these late-night visits meant a dog had been run over. Usually the dog was unconscious on the backseat when the good Samaritan arrived. Rarely could Didi save the creature.

"Is Charlie up?" she asked.

"No, miss. Should I wake him?"

"Not yet, but I may need him. Why don't you

put up some coffee, Mrs. Tunney. I'd appreciate that."

Didi opened the door. The short, stocky visitor was standing in the light rain. He was not young, maybe sixty, and wearing a fisherman's hat. He looked like one of the lost hunters who always turned up in Hillsbrook during deer season, trying unsuccessfully to read the area maps.

"Are you Dr. Nightingale?" the man asked.

"Yes. Can I help you?"

"I hope so. My name is Milo Kraft. I used to be a police officer in Atlantic City."

Didi was confused. Why was this man presenting his credentials? Where was the hurt animal? She looked past him at his vehicle. She could make out little in the darkness.

"I should have waited until morning, but I was very anxious to talk to you, face to face."

"About what?" she asked. She did not like that phrase "face to face." Her confusion escalated into uneasiness.

"About Eleazar Wynn."

Didi stepped back instinctively, her agitation rising. She thought she had successfully interred that horror. Not, obviously, deep enough. The memory burst open like an orange.

"I did not know Dr. Wynn," she said firmly.

"But you were there when he was murdered."

"Yes. I was in that shoe store in Cape May when it happened. Look, Mr. Kraft, would you like to come in out of the rain?"

"No. I'm fine. I'll finish this quickly. It concerns a valued informant of mine while I was a police officer. His name was Lucius Harmony and he was killed about eighteen months ago, just before I retired. He was murdered in a bar in exactly the same way that Wynn was murdered."

"I don't know what to say."

"I need information from you about the murder weapon. A description."

"There's nothing I can tell you. You used to be a policeman. Why not go to your former colleagues?"

"They will not release any information on the murder weapon during an ongoing investigation. That's standard police procedure."

"OK. But I never got a close look at it. You must understand. The scene was a bit chaotic."

The visitor seemed to ignore her protestations.

"The weapon that killed Lucius Harmony was a thin, hand-carved, black teak letter opener. There were strange marks painted on it a kind of design. Was the object in Wynn's neck similar?"

"I don't know, Mr. Kraft. I told you, I never really inspected it."

The rain started to come down harder. Didi stepped back into the shelter of the door. Milo Kraft didn't move. The rivulets began to run along and off the brim of his hat.

"Are you quite sure about this?" he asked. His voice had suddenly become stained with pathos.

"I can't help you, Mr. Kraft. I really can't."

And that was that. He turned and left, muttering to himself. Didi couldn't tell if he was frustrated, angry, or simply uncomfortably wet.

Chapter 4

There were only two stops on the morning rounds—a Morgan mare that had miscarried and a milk cow with a badly lacerated ear.

Then Didi drove into town and parked the Jeep.

"Meet you back here in about an hour," she said to Charlie. "I have some shopping to do."

Charlie had no shopping whatsoever to do. He meandered off, up Main Street, looking into the store windows with a practiced, rueful eye.

The part of Main Street that contained commercial establishments was only six blocks long, so when he reached the end of the strip, at the firehouse, he crossed over and headed back.

The new commercial growth in Hillsbrook was taking place on the side streets, in the old frame houses that lay north and south of Main Street. That growth was brisk, as the suburbs were inexorably overwhelming dairy cow country. There were new boutiques, hardware stores, hair cutters, and above all, restaurants. Many, many new places to eat—French, Italian, Indian, and even American.

One of those American spots was the Heirloom, which specialized in authentic early American farm dishes. It had received such superlative reviews that people came from all over Dutchess County and beyond to dine there.

That was where Charlie spotted his friend Ike Badian. Ike was staring at the restaurant front and the sign with the brunch menu.

Charlie called out to him from the street. Ike didn't acknowledge his greeting. The poor bastard is morose, thought Charlie. And why shouldn't he be? When they shut down your dairy farm after fifty-odd years, you simply don't know what the hell to do with your time.

He walked quickly down the side street and clapped his friend on the shoulder.

"What's up, Ike?"

"Nothing."

"What are you doing?"

"What does it look like I'm doing?"

"Reading the brunch menu."

The two old dairy men perused it together, squinting.

The dishes available that day were:

—Homestead skillet eggs with tomato sauce $8.95
—Scrambled French toast with bacon bits $8.95
—Scalloped parsnips and carrots $5.95
—Corn chip stuffed tomatoes $5.95
—Baked hash and poached eggs $9.95
—Baked beef heart with green peas $10.95
—Sausage with cream gravy on biscuits $10.95
—Early berries with buttermilk, brown
   sugar $6.95

Charlie stepped back and burst out laughing.

"What the hell is so funny?" Ike demanded.

"I'm old enough to be an early American farmer, Ike, or something like that. And believe me, I don't remember anyone ever cooking me food like that. Where did they get that stuff? And please tell me what an early berry is."

Ike replied: "My grandmother made me baked beef heart once. I remember."

"OK. Anyway, let's get a beer, Ike. The boss gave me an hour off."

"Don't feel like one."

"Well, you can't just stand around here and brood."

"I need money, Charlie."

"Yeah, so do I."

"All these years, Charlie, I always made fun

of you and your schemes to make money. Well, I finally appreciate what you were doing. And I apologize for making fun of you. I really do."

Charlie chuckled. This meant Ike had finally forgiven him for that last adventure. They were going to make a fortune as a comedy team. One old Samurai (Charlie) and one old cow (Ike), both in full costume, doing a Belushi-type slapstick skit about milking a cow. Oh, what a disaster it had been—including a riot at the night club where they were performing.

Ike added: "I understand your desperation now."

"Hey, Ike! Take a break. Desperation? I never suggested robbing a bank."

"Remember that movie, Charlie?"

"What movie?"

"About three old geezers who pull off a bank job."

"Oh yeah. Sounds familiar."

A beautiful young woman in waitress garb stepped out of the front door of the restaurant for a smoke.

She smiled at them. The old men nodded and moved off the side street.

*   *   *

Dr. Nightingale selected the establishment with the most magazine racks—a drugstore—and began her search methodically.

She had no idea what she was looking for. As of late, she had become an obsessional purchaser of magazines, all kinds of magazines. Once bought, they lay unread in stacks in her room. There were fashion magazines, gardening, military, science, movie, occult, even sewing magazines.

She knew dimly that it was the selection and purchase of said magazines that she had become addicted to—and she speculated that it had something to do with her financial crunch.

Today, however, her excitement over her selection was dimmed . . . dulled . . . almost nonexistent.

She studied the covers, but there was no charge, no rush.

Her mind was on that strange midnight visit by that strange man, Milo Kraft. And on his request that she identify the shape and markings of the gruesome weapon that had dispatched Dr. Wynn.

"Hello."

Didi turned. A woman stood three feet away from her. Odd-looking, about forty, dressed expensively, elegantly, but in a childlike fashion. A tall woman with brownish curls in a very chic cut.

Tears were rolling from her eyes.

"I feel so close to you," she said, snuffling.

The stranger wasn't talking about spatial proximity. That made Didi very nervous. She looked for help. There was no one else in the magazine section. Two or three customers were roaming the aisles near the pharmacy section. That was reassuring.

The woman snapped open her purse. Didi flinched, but the stranger didn't bring out a weapon, only a snapshot, which she thrust at Didi.

Didi saw a yacht. It was tied up at a marina—the Atlantic City Marina, to be precise.

There were four people in the photo, standing on the deck of the yacht. Didi recognized two of them: the tearful woman in front of her and Eleazar Wynn.

"You see!" the woman exclaimed. "We were all there for the convention." She started tapping the photo. "Me, my husband, my husband's partner, Arthur Bremen, and their foreman, Mary Alonso. We were all there. But you were the last person to see Eleazar alive! Do you understand why I feel so close to you? Do you understand!"

"Yes," Didi replied. "I think I do."

Didi noticed that the young woman in the photo, the so-called foreman, was wearing a T-shirt that read MID-FLORIDA EQUINE CLINIC. She assumed it was the corporate name of Wynn's practice.

"My name is Joy Wynn, Dr. Nightingale, and I have searched hard to identify and find you."

Didi became nervous again.

"There were other people in that shoe store," Didi noted. "Three other people who saw your husband before he was murdered."

"Yes, but this . . . you were fate. I checked with the University of Pennsylvania, where you went to vet school. They said you were a brilliant student. And that's what I need now. You see, Dr. Nightingale, my husband helped build the most successful veterinary practice in Florida, maybe in the entire eastern United States, but he was really interested only in his research. On lameness in Thoroughbreds. He had been working on a book for ten years. His joy, his ambition, his creativity, his passion was thrown into it. Now he's gone. Before he could finish it. I want you to complete it. Yes, Dr. Nightingale, it's what he would have wanted."

Didi shook her head.

"I'm flattered, Mrs. Wynn," she said, "but I doubt I'm the one you're looking for. I've been away from books for a long time, and horses were never my specialty. That's why I went to the convention. To learn."

"Please, just listen to my offer. All you have to do, really, is polish a rough draft and check sources. The whole project will take only five or six weeks—at the outside. I'll pay your transportation down and back. You'll have a beautiful office and all the secretarial help you need. And the fee will be twenty thousand dollars. Ten thousand up front. Ten thousand when you finish it."

Didi was staggered by the amount. She didn't know how to respond.

Joy Wynn said: "Please think it over. I must know by this evening. I'm staying in that bed-and-breakfast around the corner."

She headed out of the store.

"Mrs. Wynn!" Didi called out.

The elegant woman turned back.

"Do you know a man named Milo Kraft?" Didi asked.

"No. I never heard the name."

Didi noted that there were still tears in the woman's eyes.

"Don't order no whiskey, Ike. We're too old and too broke. I'm buying you just one beer."

The bartender slid the two steins in front of them.

"You ever eat in that restaurant, Charlie?"

"The Heirloom? Of course not. Do I look crazy?"

"What about your boss? She eat there?"

"I don't know. Doc doesn't have much cash lately. I don't figure she'd appreciate spending nine bucks for hash and eggs."

"What the hell happened to her practice? She was supposed to be the golden girl."

"You're out of touch, Ike. This is a hard place to be a vet now, unless you got a real busy dog and cat clinic."

"What about all the new horse-breeding operations in the county? They seem to be popping up all over."

"Doc just can't seem to get connected."

"Too young, too pretty."

"Maybe. But you know, Ike, she is a helluva vet. Particularly with cows. She is a cow lady. She has the gift."

Ike snorted in contempt. "Gift, Charlie? You're talking like an idiot. I never saw a vet, in fifty years milking, with any kind of gift. Not a one. They pump the cow full of pharmaceuticals and step back and look wise. Gift, my ass!"

"Ooh, you're getting to be a bitter old man,

Ike. Believe me, she has the gift with cows. You know the Rorty operation?"

"You mean the Greene County spread?"

"Yeah. Eighty-eight cows in a single barn. The place is so high-tech it could be exported to outer space. So, about six months ago, they call Doc . . . some kind of fever. We walk in. I'm following the doc. She's following the manager down the aisle. You won't believe what happens. All the cows . . . eighty-eight of them . . . start swishing their tails in unison. Like Doc was the conductor of the New York Philharmonic."

Ike stared incredulously at his friend and took a long drink of beer.

"It's the honest truth, Ike," Charlie said. "A goddamn milk pail serenade by cows who never saw a milk pail in their lives."

Badian lit one of his small, stubby, evil-smelling cigars after biting off the tip and spitting it onto the floor.

Suddenly Charlie looked aggrieved. "You don't do that in this kind of bar, Ike."

Badian finished his beer in one huge swallow. He wiped his mouth, pushed the stein away, swiveled on the bar stool so that he was facing Charlie directly, and said: "Do you know what really bugs me about that place?"

"What place?"

"The restaurant. The Heirloom. What kind of hash was it?"

"Baked hash, the menu said."

"Yeah. But was it corned beef hash? Or roast beef? Pork? What kind?"

"What does it matter, Ike? People with money don't need to know. They taste the hash. They like what they taste, they eat it. They don't like it, they buy another dish."

"I guess so," Ike agreed grimly. He spun on the stool so that he was once again facing the bar. He muttered something.

"Can't hear you," Gravis said, searching for a wall clock to see how much time was left before he had to return to the Jeep.

Ike spoke louder, but not by much: "You really think we can pull off a bank job, Charlie?"

"I never said nothing about robbing a bank. You were talking about an old movie."

"Was I?"

Didi had dropped Charlie off at the house and driven to see her friend.

Now she was lying on one of the large woven mats that softened the dirt floor of Rose Vigdor's perpetually unfinished barn dwelling.

The two German shepherds and the corgi were delighted to see her. They were all over her—

climbing and licking and growling playfully. Her boots were particularly sought after.

Rose was brewing tea on her antique wood-burning stove, the one that had almost burned down the barn—four times; the one that Rose had refused to abandon.

The cups were huge and bizarrely decorated. The tea was Rose's special blend—half camomile, half cranberry.

Did took the proffered cup and went into the lotus position. The dogs ran off. Rose sat down on a reinforced milk crate.

"You've lost weight," Didi noted, "and you've let your hair grow."

Rose grinned, shook out her blond hair, stood up, and did a pirouette, surprisingly supple for a large woman who had just spent a winter cooped up and freezing. Then she sat down. "Us blondes always have more fun," she said, adjusting her Guatemalan-style cape.

She leaned forward, her hands around the cup.

"Guess who I met in town, Nightingale."

"Charlie Gravis?"

"No. Allie Voegler."

Didi didn't reply.

"Your officer Voegler was friendly, believe it or not. In his own special way, of course. He actually asked me how the dogs were doing. Then he invited me to have a drink with him."

A smidgen of tension suddenly pervaded the spacious barn.

"And?"

"Of course I didn't."

"You could have, you know. You're a free woman, Rose. So is he. A free *man*, I mean—well, you know what I mean."

"He's not my cup of tea, Nightingale."

"But he is mine?"

"Well, he was."

"We all make mistakes."

Didi laughed. The tension dissolved.

"What else is going on, Nightgown?"

Didi sipped her tea and smiled.

"About an hour ago, in town, a stranger walked up to me and offered me twenty-thousand dollars in cash for five weeks' work."

"Well, I hope you told him you don't turn tricks, even if it's on a yacht bound for Majorca."

Didi smiled, a bit grimly. Rose was her best friend in Hillsbrook, maybe her only friend, but their conversations were never the intense, intimate dialogues friends were supposed to have, like the ones in novels.

No, they were short, laconic, filled with quips. And the confidences were always somehow coded. Of course, each of them easily cracked the other's code, but Didi was always left with the feeling that she had shortchanged her friend and that she, in turn, had been shortchanged.

Didi took the blame for this. It was, she assumed, the way her excruciating shyness as a child manifested itself in adulthood.

It was odd, she realized, that she had often discussed intimate matters with Allie Voegler even though she had not considered him a friend. That was difficult to understand. He had been her lover, and almost her husband, but never a friend. And that was, no doubt, the reason their on-again off-again relationship had terminated.

Her relationships with men had taken on a perverse logic.

To the one man she had loved—the professor in vet school—she had revealed intimacies. He, also, was not a friend.

Yet she would have followed him to the ends of the earth.

Not Allie, however, although the relationship had been logically the same: sex, conversational intimacy, but no friendship.

The wild card was love. She obviously had not loved Allie. And she would follow him nowhere.

So she was alone again. Except for Rose, God bless her.

"Not a 'he,' Rose," she answered. "The offer came from a woman. And the money is for polishing up a manuscript. I'd have to go to Florida to do the work. You remember what I told you about that murder in the Cape May shoe store?"

"Yes."

"The man who was killed . . . it was his widow who made me the offer."

"What's the manuscript—*War and Peace*?"

"Just a monograph, it seems, on lameness in Thoroughbred racing horses."

Rose arched her eyebrows. "You sure she was talking about American money?"

"Indeed. Cash. Half immediately. The other half when I finish. She'll pay transportation costs. And room and board."

"So what are you going to do?"

"It's a bad time of year to leave my practice, but I don't think I can refuse. It'll get me out of debt. It's enough money to give me a cushion."

Whap! Something hit Didi in the face. She lost her lotus position and fell over backward. Then she burst out laughing. Rose had flung at her one of the ubiquitous cushions that littered the straw mats.

Chapter 5

Mrs. Tunney was preparing lunch—noodles with cottage cheese and butter. Not just for herself; not just for all the elves; for *everyone*. Including Miss Quinn.

Now, this was unheard of: the doctor eating with all of them in the kitchen. At her specific request.

Mrs. Tunney found it more than peculiar. It was disturbing.

Obviously it meant an announcement of some sort was in the offing.

But what?

At two minutes before noon, Charlie walked in and sat down. The noodles would be ready at seven minutes past. Mrs. Tunney cooked them soft.

Abigail came in. Then a surly Trent Tucker. Well, Mrs. Tunney thought, at least everyone is here. At least we'll all get the news at the same time.

Upstairs, Dr. Nightingale made her last-minute preparations. The car service would pick her up at 2 P.M. for the drive into Manhattan and Penn Station.

On the bed was one suitcase, packed and shut. The open attaché case next to it contained the rough draft of the manuscript Joy Wynn had given her the night before, when Didi had gone to the bed-and-breakfast place in town to accept the assignment.

Earlier that morning Didi had met Mrs. Wynn for breakfast at the Hillsbrook Diner. It was Mrs. Wynn who had made a roomette reservation for her on the 8:35 P.M. Silver Streak, which would pull into Orlando twenty-four hours later. A van from the Mid-Florida Equine establishment would be waiting for her.

Joy Wynn had announced that she'd made plane reservations for Didi—Delta. But when the young vet remarked that she preferred trains to all other modes of transportation, and that she loved long-distance trains best of all, the widow made the change, merely noting: "If time is no factor to you . . . well, then . . ."

After breakfast they'd gone to Didi's bank, where Mrs. Wynn, using some ultramodern combination computer/wire transaction, had transferred into Didi's account the first part of the payment: $10,000.

Didi had then cashed a check for $3,000 and taken half of that in traveler's checks.

Now she picked up the five envelopes that lay on the bed next to the attaché case.

Four of them were small white #10 envelopes. The fifth was a large manila envelope.

She left the bedroom, descended the stairs, and walked quickly down the hall and into the kitchen.

Mrs. Tunney was mixing the cottage cheese and butter into the noodles in a huge bowl.

Dr. Nightingale hesitated. Why were these people such a problem to her? Why did she always feel so uncomfortable in their presence?

To a great extent the discomfort was based on the fact that they forced her to feel as if she were some kind of lord of the manor and they were her serfs.

After all, they received no salaries, only room and board in exchange for running the house and maintaining the property.

When she had returned home to practice veterinary medicine after her mother's death, she had had no idea they would be part of her inheritance.

Of course, for as long as she could remember, her mother had always collected stray animals and stray people—feeding them, housing them, caring for them.

During the last seven years of her mother's life, when Didi had been in school and then traveling, she had returned to Hillsbrook only once a year, at most.

One of those years, Mrs. Tunney had shown up, and never left.

Then Charlie Gravis had arrived. Followed by Trent Tucker. Then Abigail. Didi's mother had never explained their presence and Didi had assumed they were short-term strays.

Three out of her four elves were vaguely related by blood, but Didi could never remember which was which.

When she came to take over the house and property, she could have gotten rid of them all. But she hadn't; for both selfish and compassionate reasons.

Now it was too late. Even if she wanted them gone, not least because they were a financial drain, she had neither the heart nor the will to kick them out.

Still worse, she simply had never learned how to play lord of the manor properly.

It was equally bad that she could not connect

in any way with the two elves who were near her in age.

Trent Tucker was very much the Hillsbrook rowdy, the kind of boy Didi had despised while growing up. In fact, he had many of the qualities she found so objectionable in Allie Voegler.

As for Abigail . . . well, she was a very strange young woman. Most people thought she was not playing with a full deck. She rarely spoke. She rarely exhibited anger or joy. The only things she ever seemed to do with any emotion were sing in the church choir and tend to the yard dogs, Charlie Gravis's pigs, and Didi's horse. Once in a while she would get into a dreadfully inappropriate relationship with a man. Always brief and always ending badly.

Yes, the elves, as a group and individually, were a cross to bear. And every time Didi found it was too heavy and that she'd have to shrug it off, great waves of guilt washed over her. She was convinced that the mere thought of turning the elves out sent her mother gyrating in the grave.

Didi took a place at the table and the food was served. They ate in silence, heartily, except for Didi, who just picked at the noodles, to Mrs. Tunney's dismay. She pushed the salt and pepper toward the doctor, who decided it was time to act.

"I want to talk to all of you," she announced.

The elves put down their forks and chewed up what they had in their mouths. Didi gave them a few moments to finish before she continued:

"I am leaving this evening by train for Florida, from Manhattan. I will be away for five weeks, more or less. It's a well-paying assignment that I just can't afford to pass up at this time. Of course I'll be calling all of you from down there."

She handed the large manilla envelope to Charlie and explained: "Here are the names and telephone numbers of four local vets clipped together. They will be covering for me. Any calls you get, Charlie, refer them to one of the four. All of them are in general practice, so it won't be difficult. They can all handle any kind of situation. But for emergencies, refer people to Randazzo. I also put about ten case history sheets in there—animals on maintenance medication. These you are to monitor yourself. There's a separate sheet with my address and phone number in Florida. If something comes up that you simply can't handle yourself, call me. OK?"

"No problem."

"Good. Now I have something for each of you."

She distributed one of the small white envelopes to each of the elves. "Open them!" she ordered.

Abigail looked stunned when she pulled out the crisp one-hundred-dollar bill.

Trent Tucker held his up to the light and turned it over and over.

Mrs. Tunney didn't pull hers all the way out of the envelope. She looked embarrassed.

Only Charlie Gravis spoke, shaking the bill briskly. "You know, I can't remember the last time I had a hundred."

"A very late Christmas present," Didi explained.

There was an awkward silence. Trent Tucker seemed desirous of returning to his noodles. Finally Abigail asked, "Do you want me to ride Promise Me while you're gone?"

"Yes. As often as you think he needs it."

Didi waited for more questions . . . but there were none.

Rose Vigdor noticed the clock on the wall in the butcher shop as she placed her order for ten pounds of the cheapest skirt steak, five pounds of organ meats, and one pound of liver.

It was two in the afternoon. Didi was, she realized, on her way to New York City. Rose had offered to drive her, but Didi didn't trust the indomitable Vigdor Volvo. With good cause.

Rose felt herself slipping into a depression. She always did in the spring. Nice weather depressed her. It was the wrong time for her friend to abandon her.

She paid for the meat and listened to the butcher, whose name was Ray Arnheim, bemoan one of his kid's most recent indiscretions. Then she walked out onto Main Street.

The package was as heavy as it was expensive.

She would have to start rationing her beasts—maybe even cut their repasts with inexpensive dry dog food.

The idea made her wince. She was a vegetarian, but she fed her dogs according to the teachings of an Englishwoman who had once written a book stating that there was only one way to feed a dog properly: raw meat must be buried in the ground until it was half rotted, then dug up and served with cooked cereal such as oatmeal and fresh chopped greens like spinach or kale.

As Rose was contemplating the horror of a food crisis, someone pulled suddenly at her package.

She kept her grip on it . . . fought back . . . and screamed.

"What the hell is the matter with you?"

She looked up. It was Allie Voegler.

"This isn't New York City, Rose. This is Hillsbrook. Do you know where the hell you are? We don't get muggings here. I was just trying to help you with your package!"

She was dreadfully embarrassed. She handed over the package, muttering something about being lost in thought. Then she added, "I'm just going to my car."

"Isn't it funny," he remarked. "Whenever I see you in town, you're carrying something to your car."

"I don't find anything funny about that, Allie."

"Don't call me Allie. Call me Albert." Voegler laughed. "Suddenly the name 'Allie' doesn't fit me anymore. You know what I mean?"

"Not really."

Actually she did have an inkling as to why he now wanted to be Albert.

When she lived and worked in Manhattan, she had once done a PR job for a doctor who was publishing a book on alcoholism. She had been forced to read the book, and one of the symptoms identified was "alcoholic flight."

The alcoholic, desperate to escape his addiction, changes name, address, clothing . . . anything and everything . . . in the delusional belief that the need for booze will vanish too.

These changes can be incredibly trivial.

Was that what was going on here? Maybe. She couldn't be sure.

The book said that this symptom was usually present only in persons with advanced alcoholism; and she was sure that Albert aka Allie was not that advanced. After all, the man seemed to be functioning.

They reached the beat-up green Volvo. Albert rested the package on a fender. The dogs inside started going berserk.

"Word has it that Didi has shipped out again," he said matter-of-factly, "and this time for a few weeks."

Rose stiffened. Did he want her to become an informer? On her best friend? Then she remembered that Didi didn't seem to care who knew about her departure. It was no secret.

She merely nodded in affirmation.

"Listen, Rose, why don't we get that drink now?"

She didn't answer.

"Why don't you let me dump the bag in the car for you and we'll go get a burger and a beer . . . or whatever you want." His tone was urgent.

She stood there silently, evaluating the situation.

First of all, if she did as he suggested, the dogs would smell the meat and rip the package to shreds; the package would have to be put into the trunk and the trunk was not easy to open.

Second, wouldn't it be breaking the rules? What rules? Didi was through with Albert Voegler. Or so she said. Even if she was through with him, why even dabble in the mess?

Besides, she didn't like Allie—Albert—Voegler and he didn't like her.

Why drink with him? Why break bread with him? Why socialize with him at all?

Third, there was something about this man, over and above his predatory characteristics, that disturbed her, though she couldn't identify the parameters of the disturbance.

She shook her head.

Why was she compiling this fractured list in her head? Why was she carrying on so over one lousy lunch? She was hungry—but not for a burger. Maybe a salad with rich, deep blue cheese dressing.

She fiddled with the trunk lock until it opened. Albert put the bag inside gingerly. She noticed the bulge of a holster on his belt under the flannel shirt. Why the hell do they need a plainclothes cop in Hillsbrook, anyway? she asked herself.

Rose and Albert went to the fancy new pub and slid into a booth.

They ordered. Quickly the situation became awkward.

"How are you feeling?" Rose asked, trying to ease the mood.

It was a mistake. Voegler interpreted it as a reference to his recent department-ordered psychological counseling.

"There's nothing wrong with me!" he snapped.

"There's something wrong with everyone," she replied in a consoling manner.

He twirled the soda bottle between his palms as if trying to ignite a fire with sticks. That gesture, and his obvious discomfort at her question, seemed to make Rose feel kindly toward him.

"Now, take me," she announced. "I get depressed in the spring, when the weather gets nice. Isn't that ridiculous?"

"Maybe we're birds of a feather," he said, looking straight at her, hard, inquiringly.

I should get out of here right now, she thought. Then her salad was served. And his hamburger.

When the meal was over, they slid out of the

booth and, in an oddly formal fashion, shook hands, as if they had just concluded a business lunch.

Dr. Nightingale arrived in Manhattan two and a half hours before her train was scheduled to depart. She went into Macy's and bought two pairs of fancy stone-washed jeans that purported to be "work" clothes. These, she needed. She also purchased a beautiful light gray goat's hair pullover. And a pair of genuine leather driving gloves—the kind auto racers wear. She had no idea why she'd made this latter purchase except for the cliché that the money was burning a hole in her pocket.

Fifteen minutes before departure, she boarded the train and settled into her tiny roomette.

What a wonderful monk's cell, she thought. It had a comfortable chair that converted into a bed; a wardrobe and a luggage rack; a toilet; and a very large window.

There was a curtain that could be pulled across the entrance to the room, shutting one off from the activity in the corridor even if one didn't close the sliding door.

She settled in. It had been a very long time since she'd taken a long train trip in a sleeper car on one of Amtrak's best trains.

All kinds of good feelings suddenly washed over her. Excitement. Childish anticipation.

And wonder—yes, it was wonder. Like a child opening a new book filled with delightful illustrations.

There was also a peculiar sense of freedom, as if all minor problems had been solved.

Both the curtain and the sliding door were open, so she could see other passengers making their way down the aisle. Who took the train to Florida anymore? Didi tried to figure. People frightened of flying. People with kids. Those nostalgic for the past. Train buffs. People like her, who had to have a monk's cell to work on a manuscript.

She reached for the attaché case, but suddenly withdrew her hand. No, not now, she thought. After Washington, D.C. I'll start it then and work straight through. I won't even bother turning the seat down into a bed.

Yes, she'd work the twenty or so hours from D.C. to Jacksonville and then sleep until Orlando. It was a good game plan.

The conductor came by and collected her ticket.

Then the female porter came in, introduced herself, and gave Didi the times of the three meals she would be having en route. She also provided a breakfast menu for the coming morning.

The train pulled out of Penn Station, chugged through the tunnel, and burst onto the Jersey swamps. The night was dark, pierced by only a sliver of moon and a few stars.

Didi settled back in the seat. She decided to wait until Wilmington to go to the club car and get a cup of coffee and a ham and cheese sandwich. She always loved Amtrak's ham and cheese.

The open attaché case lay on top of the toilet cover, the manuscript clearly visible. It was large—divided into three sections, with a rubber band around each one.

Didi's work plan for the train ride was simply to read the manuscript slowly and make notes. Mrs. Wynn had stated that it was essentially finished in rough draft and merely had to be polished. The notes and references, however, were in a primitive state, and organizing them would be one of Didi's main tasks. A bibliography would also be required. Didi could handle notes, references, and bibliography—if Eleazar Wynn's material was as accessible as his wife claimed.

The book would also need an index. This Didi could not do. She intended to hire an indexer.

Whatever she could contribute, the price for the work seemed exorbitant. Twenty thousand dollars? Maybe grief had deranged Joy Wynn.

Didi reached over and slammed shut the top of the attaché case. Then she closed the window curtain halfway and the sliding door to the corridor all the way, and relaxed once again.

The train pulled into Newark, where it picked up more passengers.

She turned off the overhead light.

The train pulled in and out of the Metro Park station. A few more passengers came and went.

Didi continued to enjoy the ride as the train picked up speed on the run to Trenton. All kinds of music popped into her head. Train music. Patsy Cline music. Johnny Cash music. Cow music. But nary a CD in sight.

Grinning like a child, she grasped the armrests and went with the rhythm of the wheels. The Donkey Serenade.

The train pulled into the long, gloomy Trenton station. She peered out the window in both directions. No one seemed to be getting on or off.

She was getting edgy. Maybe she wouldn't wait until Wilmington to visit the club car. Maybe she'd do it after the next stop—Philadelphia.

She settled back. Only a half hour between

Trenton and Philly. The music in her head had terminated.

Soon the train entered the run through the blighted industrial outskirts of North Philadelphia. She always found this stretch as fascinating as it was sad. There seemed to be hundreds of huge abandoned factories with broken windows . . . millions of smashed frames.

Didi finally closed the view out the simplest way possible—she shut her eyes. She concentrated her thoughts on her elves. How would each of them spend the gift?

Mrs. Tunney, she knew, wouldn't spend a dime of it. Abigail? Well, that was difficult. Perhaps . . .

She got no further in her speculations.

The train lurched violently. She was thrown halfway out of her seat. Rising and grabbing the overhead rack, she steadied herself.

Then the train made three small disturbing bounces.

And came to a dead stop.

She heard people shouting in the aisle. She heard a man bellowing: "Someone pulled the emergency cord!"

She heard a woman yell out: "Nothing's wrong. For God's sake, nothing's wrong!"

All the lights in the train went out.

Didi could see through her window that there were figures on the embankment beside the train.

The shouting in the aisle subsided, but she heard people moving quickly. She stuck her head out.

"Take all your stuff!" an Asian man told her.

It was obvious the train was being emptied. Probably the emergency stop had damaged something.

Didi grabbed her suitcase, attaché case, and jacket. She joined the other passengers in the exodus, helped down the last steep step by the conductor and porter who were stationed on either side of the door.

A man appeared on the embankment with a megaphone.

"All passengers are being bused into the Thirtieth Street Station in Philadelphia. Please walk to the rear of the train. There's a path to the road where the buses will be pulling up. Train personnel will help all those who cannot carry their luggage. Please walk slowly. Walk to the rear of the train."

All around her, people began to talk. One said a man had fallen from the train. Another said the emergency stop had burned out the undercarriage. There were all kinds of rumors.

Didi joined the others shuffling along the embankment toward the place where the buses would be arriving. The ground was rugged, but train personnel had put out emergency flares to light the way.

The flares cast eerie flickering shadows on the demobilized passengers, who seemed to be walking toward the abandoned industrial section of North Philadelphia. They looked like refugees from an old war heading back to their bombed-out city.

A small group of men huddled together on the embankment, appearing to be warming their hands around a fire.

Didi moved on.

As she passed the circle of men, she saw an object on the ground.

A hat.

Not a conductor's hat.

No. Not at all.

A fisherman's hat.

She stepped quickly out of line and approached the object.

One of the trainmen called out: "Leave that alone, miss! Please get back with the others!"

Her legs began to tremble. She recognized that hat.

She walked toward the center of the circle of men.

An engineer with a lantern barred her way. It didn't matter.

Didi could see the dead body of Milo Kraft.

Contorted. Pale. One leg twisted crazily.

A slim black object was buried in his neck.

"Get back now! I'm warning you!"

This time Didi complied. But she didn't go back to the line of marchers. She scrambled farther up on the embankment. She had trouble catching her breath.

Everything started to spin. What was happening? What was going on? How was it possible?

Didi tried to steady herself and gather her wits. She turned away from the circle of mourners, if that was what they were.

Then she caught a glimpse of something white along the embankment.

It seemed to be moving, to be beckoning her. She stood and took several tentative steps toward it.

Her eyes focused.

She saw a little white lamb tethered to an upright stick in the ground. Tethered by its back foot. The tether itself seemed to be a plain clothesline. The lamb was silent, not bleating, hardly moving. It looked well and content.

Am I crazy? she thought. This is North

Philadelphia, not a village in Greece. There are no lambs pasturing here. There are no shepherds to tether them.

She rushed down the embankment to join the others.

Twenty minutes later, she was seated on a bench in the 30th Street Station.

She found it odd that she'd been sitting on the same bench in the same railroad station only a few days before, on her way to the convention.

It was odder still that Milo Kraft had been on that Florida train.

Oddest of all was that he had been murdered in the exact same way as his informer, Lucien Harmony. The exact same way as Eleazar Wynn, the man whose death he was investigating in his visit to Didi.

I am next, Didi thought. I am going to be murdered next.

Was that not what was waiting for her in Florida? An object rammed into that delicate artery in her neck?

She tried to think clearly. A *place* kept popping up.

Milo Kraft had said he was a retired Atlantic City police officer.

Eleazar Wynn had been murdered in Cape

May while attending a convention in Atlantic City.

The yacht in the photo that Joy Wynn had tearfully shown her was tied up at an Atlantic City marina.

Kraft's informer had also been killed in Atlantic City.

Didi suddenly checked her wallet. The cash and traveler's checks were intact. Why did she think it would be otherwise?

The lamb! She remembered that little white tethered lamb. Had that been a hallucination?

She slipped into an exhausted half-sleep.

But she kept hearing train wheels. How could that be! She was sitting in the station.

Then she saw that ghostly white lamb again, in her mind's eye.

Was it an omen? Was it a sign that she was being hunted?

Doctor Nightingale didn't believe in omens.

So why did she believe that she would be "next"?

Because, she realized, she had taken a profound misstep and had fallen into something horrible. She had fallen—nay, hurtled—and was in free fall.

It was, as her mother used to say, "as plain as the egg on your face."

Milo Kraft had come to see her about a murder she had witnessed and a murder she had not. He had died following her. She would be next.

Her metaphor, she realized, had been wrong. She had not really "fallen" into a murderous stew—she was being lowered on a chain.

And the links of the chain were letter openers, lambs, manuscripts, and corpses.

Oh, there was no doubt she was the next corpse.

Or was she simply collapsing under the weight of events, of financial stress, of love lost, of a practice that had not flowered?

Was she having a nervous breakdown?

What pathetic drivel! she thought. I know what I know.

She was wide awake now.

One question was paramount. Where was she safe?

Not in Florida. Not going to Florida.

Florida was the periphery.

The wolf pack hunts on the periphery, selecting lambs who stray from the flock.

She was safer in the center of the flock . . . in the center of the storm.

Only in the center could she see where the chain was going and whence it had come.

Only in the center could she cut the chain.

An announcement was made twenty minutes

before midnight. New equipment for the Florida-bound passengers would be arriving in about twenty minutes.

Didi's roomette in the new equipment would remain vacant.

Five minutes before the passengers reboarded, Didi climbed onto the train called the Gambler's Special. Destination: Atlantic City.

Ike Badian parked his pickup truck illegally on Main Street, rolled down the window, and shouted to Charlie Gravis, who was pacing impatiently: "OK. I'm here!"

"What the hell took you so long?"

"What's the rush? Where are you going?"

"To buy lottery tickets."

"Are you crazy, Charlie? You got me into town to watch you buy a lottery ticket?"

Charlie walked over to the pickup and thrust the hundred-dollar bill through the window.

"First," he announced, "we'll get a whole lot of tickets. Then I'm buying us a steak."

Ike exited the vehicle. "Where'd you get the hundred?"

"Does Macy's tell Gimbel's?" Gravis retorted as they headed for the stationery store that sold most of the lottery tickets in town.

"There ain't no Gimbel's anymore, Charlie."

The two entered the store and stood in front of the counter.

"What are you playing? Pick-Six?"

"What are *we* playing," Charlie corrected. "I'm cutting you in for half."

Charlie slapped the bill on the counter and ordered twenty-five $2 Win For Life scratch-off tickets.

The lady vendor grinned, held the bill up to the light to check its authenticity, and began to count off the tickets from a roll.

"What do we win?" Badian asked.

"One thousand dollars a week for as long as we live ... I think," said Charlie, pocketing the tickets and the change.

They walked to the upscale Hillsbrook Pub, sat at the bar, ordered two rib-eye steaks with mashed potatoes, two ales, two rye whiskeys, and utilizing dimes supplied by Charlie, they began the laborious task of scratching out the cards.

"We lost," Ike announced when the last ticket came up blank.

"So what? Soon there'll be a lot more where that came from."

"What are you talking about, Charlie?"

The food arrived. The two dairy farmers ate with precision and gusto. They cleaned the last morsels from their plates and wiped up the garlicked mashed potato gravy with exotic bite-size rolls. The small side salads were consumed as dessert.

Finished, Ike lit a cigar.

Charlie sat back expansively on the high, deep stool. "I had a vision," he announced.

"Hallelujah!" Ike snorted sarcastically.

Charlie ignored the insult.

"In this vision, Ike, I saw your beautiful old barn . . . so big . . . so empty . . . so unproductive now. Then I saw it sort of transformed. Inside were beautiful old chairs and tables made of thick wood. There were crisp white linen tablecloths. In the vision, it was evening. Not late. And dozens of fancy cars were pulling up to your barn.

"Yes, people had come from all over—some of them had been driving for hours. Why? To sit down at those tables, pay big money, and eat a long-lost, newly rediscovered American farm cuisine that had recently become all the rage.

"Yes, Ike, they want to eat authentic Hillsbrook farm food. Dishes of such finger-licking excellence and bouquet . . . dishes so hearty that the diner is transported back to when this land along the Hudson was a Garden of Eden."

There was silence.

"Well?" Charlie demanded.

"I definitely need another whiskey," Ike noted.

Chapter 6

Dr. Nightingale woke up. The first thing she saw was a clock radio on a small table beside the bed.

She was confused. The clock read twelve on the dot. It couldn't be midnight; the place was flooded with sunlight. Could it be noon? She had never slept until noon in her life.

She got up from the bed and walked quickly to the window. There was the street, one floor below, and a large building across the way. Turning her head, she saw water. My God! It was the ocean.

Then she remembered exactly where she was—in a motel room in Atlantic City.

She dressed and walked one block to the boardwalk. It was a lovely day. There was a cart that sold coffee and edibles. She was suddenly starved. She ate three old-fashioned donuts and drank two large coffees while sitting on a bench.

In front of her was the Atlantic Ocean, behind her the casinos flung out along the boardwalk. Didi realized her motel was incongruously nestled between two of them.

The memory of Milo Kraft's fate came to her full force as she sat there. She felt stupid, impotent, and frightened.

What was she doing eating donuts?

As of late, in fact, she had been eating an inordinate number of donuts—jelly, glazed, plain, old-fashioned. It seemed to have emerged as one of her staple foods. She knew this bizarre behavior had something to do with Allie Voegler. While he was suspended from the Hillsbrook P.D. and undergoing psychiatric treatment at Basset Hospital in Cooperstown, she'd felt obliged to meet him once or twice a week halfway between there and Hillsbrook.

They always met in a donut shop on Route 28. It was an uncomfortable situation. For both of them. The relationship was unraveling.

They sat and talked nonsense and ate donuts. That was where this ridiculous donut fetish had begun. At least two donuts for her at each meeting.

Why was it continuing?

She hadn't the slightest idea. Unless it was

simply a craving for sugar and the quick jolts of energy it could provide.

She went back to the motel and sat, no, almost crouched on the bed. She had to construct a plan, a program of action.

First, of course, she had to notify the Mid-Florida Equine Clinic that when the train pulled into Orlando this evening, she would not be on it.

She made the call. A clinic assistant answered. Didi gave him a message for Joy Wynn: Dr. Nightingale would be a few days late and would inform her shortly of the exact date of arrival.

If Mrs. Wynn was planning on murdering her, she would be a bit disappointed at the cancellation.

After the call, she pulled the manuscript out of the attaché case and began to read it.

The Introduction was pedestrian, not at all what she had expected. Wynn stated that the reason he was writing his book was that he had become aware through his practice of the persistence of archaic and harmful modes of treatment among trainers of racehorses. One of the examples he presented was the use of steroids and the firing iron to treat the ubiquitous "bucked shins" syndrome. These forms of treatment, he noted, only masked the pain but did not deal with the lesion.

Didi began to flip through the pages of the manuscript.

It was essentially a practical manual on the causes, symptoms, and treatments for all types of lameness.

There were, it seemed to Didi, only two aspects of the book that differentiated it from other such manuals.

First, there was a heavy concentration on the actual mechanics of the equine locomotor system—with illustrations of muscles, bones, joints, tendons, and ligaments subjected to inputs such as gravity.

In addition, there were many actual case histories taken from Wynn's own practice.

Didi dropped the manuscript suddenly, as if it were plague-drenched.

First donuts and now a manuscript.

What the hell was the matter with her? She was in danger. In great danger. From whom, she couldn't be sure. Why, she had no idea.

She lay down on the bed. It had been made up during her short walk to the boardwalk. She wondered what kind of pain she would feel when that thin letter-opener-type weapon was thrust into her carotid artery. How, really, did one die?

Did one feel, sense, actually experience the blood loss—the splattering geyser gush? Did one go immediately into shock? She knew the book wisdom on arteries. But what about the real living-dying victim? She knew all too well that veterinary science had nothing to do with a dying horse, with the real beast suffering and dying.

She stared at the ceiling.

What should she do next?

Count the corpses with letter openers in their necks? Lucien Harmony. Eleazar Wynn. Milo Kraft.

Others might be in danger—not counting herself.

Maybe the others in the shoe store.

She sat up, alarmed. She must warn that eccentric young woman who had befriended her at the convention: Ann Huggins.

She picked up the phone and called Toronto Information.

There was no Ann Huggins in the professional and business listings for veterinarians. There were two Ann Hugginses in the residential listings.

Didi called them both.

The first was an elderly woman. The second was not at home, but the female voice on the answering machine had a pronounced West Indian accent.

Didi then obtained from Toronto Information the names and numbers of five dog and cat hospitals and clinics in the area. She called each of them. No one had ever heard of a vet in Toronto named Ann Huggins.

This was profoundly disturbing.

She called the house in Hillsbrook. Mrs. Tunney answered. The old woman was confused. "You calling from the train, Miss Quinn?"

"No, I'm not on the train. I'm in Atlantic City. I stopped off for a day or two en route."

"Are you sick, miss?"

"No. Not at all. But if you receive any calls, don't tell anyone where I am. It's our secret, Mrs. Tunney."

She hung up, walked to the window, and stared out at the looming casino. At least she'd be able to get a meal there.

Her nervousness, she realized, was increasing. She was getting nowhere. What was her logical next step?

No doubt about it. She sat down on the bed again and called Craig Nova, the New Jersey State Trooper homicide detective. He wasn't there. She left a message.

A gull flashed by outside the window, heading toward the water. It *was* a gull, wasn't it? Like the tethered lamb, she thought, like Ann Huggins, it may or may not exist.

What is going on? Rose Vigdor thought. Is it just a series of coincidences, or is he stalking me?

This time she met Albert Voegler as she walked out of the large Agway store north of town and headed for the parking lot.

She heard him before she saw him.

"No purchase?" he asked mockingly.

He was seated in his car, the window open, one arm dangling out as though he was signaling a left turn.

"No purchase," she affirmed, slowing but not stopping.

"What were you looking for?"

She stopped then. "A .22 caliber rifle."

He laughed. "I thought you were a pacifist."

"You don't know anything about me."

"Who are you going to shoot?"

"Rats. At the drain near the road by my barn. The dogs think they're woodchucks and go for them. Sooner or later they're going to run into a car."

"Why don't you use poison?"

"I'd rather shoot them."

"Poison is surer and cheaper."

"Look! I try not to eat chemicals. So why would I inject chemicals into the ground, even if rats live there?"

She paused, then added, "Besides, poison kills slowly. I'm not in the rat torture business."

"Have you ever handled a .22 before?"

"No," she admitted, and noticed that his eyes had fixed on the side mirror.

She turned to see what was being reflected. Trent Tucker was standing in front of the store with two friends. They were all smoking and laughing.

"Are they under surveillance?" she asked incredulously.

"Not at this time."

"Trent Tucker's a sweet kid," Rose said. "Sometimes he gets a bit wild, but nothing too bad."

"Sweet? Yeah, like a pit bull."

"Oh, come on, Officer Voegler," she chided. "You just have it in for all of Didi's elves."

"Why shouldn't I? They're spongers. They drain her dry. Didi supports the whole lot of them. If I was living there, I would send them packing in five minutes."

"Maybe that's why you're not living there."

"What the hell does that mean?"

She didn't answer. She waved her hand, signifying that the conversation was futile, and walked on, heading for the Volvo.

He jumped out of the car, shouting: "Wait! Goddamn it, wait a minute!"

Rose halted in her tracks, turned.

"Do you really think those people have Didi's best interests at heart?" he demanded.

"As much as you do."

"I loved her!"

"Past tense?" she queried.

"Past, present, and future. Who the hell knows? Things just happened. And you were partly responsible, weren't you? You can't afford to throw any stones, honey."

Stones? Rose bristled. But she knew what he was talking about. Voegler's troubles had commenced during an intense murder investigation. The victim had been a Hillsbrook police officer named Wynton Chung. She had had a brief, passionate, rather innocent affair with Chung shortly before he was murdered. For some odd reason Albert Voegler had blamed her, in part, for Chung's death.

"What a fool you are!" she said.

"Am I?"

"A one hundred percent dyed-in-the-wool Yankee Doodle kind of fool."

"But I thought people like you suffered fools gladly."

"Who are these 'people like you'?" she said hotly.

"You know."

"No, Voegler, I don't."

"Weird, beautiful women," he said.

Rose had no answer for that remark. She walked quickly to her car. She was profoundly discomfitted.

Dr. Nightingale didn't leave the motel room. She waited for the homicide detective. He arrived just before seven in the morning, dressed as if he had been interrupted painting a kitchen. His eyes no longer seemed hooded.

Craig Nova sat down on the only chair in the room and began opening a bag on his lap.

"This is my supper. A grilled cheese sandwich. You want half, Dr. Nightingale?"

"No, thanks."

"You look frightened."

"I am."

He unwrapped the sandwich, opened a Pepsi can, took one bite and one sip, then said simply, "OK. Talk to me."

Didi sat down on the bed.

"Detective Nova, do you have any suspects in the Eleazar Wynn murder?"

He burst out laughing. "Do you mean you got me here to interrogate me?"

"No, I asked you here to tell you a story."

"I'm all ears," he said, taking another bite of the sandwich.

Didi spoke for forty minutes. She told him everything she remembered about her meetings with Joy Wynn and Milo Kraft in Hillsbrook. She gave him every detail she recalled about the murder on the train. The only thing she did not mention was the tethered lamb. Just thinking about it made her uncomfortable, embarrassed, unsure as to exactly what she had seen and whether it meant anything at all.

When she was finished, Nova pulled out a small pad and a ballpoint pen.

"Give me those names again," he said. "I mean, the ex-cop and the dead snitch, if that's what he was."

"The policeman was named Milo Kraft. The informant was Lucien Harmony."

"Spell out the last name."

"H-A-R-M-O-N-Y. As in—as in *harmony*, I suppose."

He nodded.

"Tell me, Dr. Nightingale, do you think Joy

Wynn should be a suspect in her husband's murder?"

"I really don't know."

"But you're afraid of her, aren't you?"

"I—I'm afraid to go to Florida," she stammered. "I believe I've gotten into something that I can't handle."

Nova smiled. "Would you please step out of the room for about ten minutes? I have to make some calls."

Her anger flared. "May I remind you, this is my room and that is my phone."

He smiled again.

Didi walked out the door and began to pace up and down the second-floor balcony. She could hear the ocean. The lights from the casino were like berserk beams sweeping up and down the street.

When she walked back in, Nova was sitting in the chair scribbling on his notepad.

"Sit down," he said firmly. Didi obeyed.

"The Kraft murder is not in my jurisdiction, Doctor. It's Philly P.D. But Kraft was not lying to you. He was a retired Atlantic City police officer. And his suspicion was correct. The weapon in the still-unsolved Lucien Harmony murder in Atlantic City two years ago was the same kind of thing that killed the vet, and probably Kraft himself.

"It was a very thin black steel letter opener. There was a series of small circles painted on it. The kind of freebie a lot of companies use as advertising gimmicks—some inexpensive object with the name of the firm printed on it. You know . . . their salesmen give them out to customers. But we have been unable to trace the one used in the Wynn murder."

Didi shivered. What he told her sounded like the stories she used to hear about swine flu epidemics before there were rigorous diagnostic tests. There were only symptoms that seemed to match each other . . . reproduce each other . . . like letter openers sticking out of necks. And symptoms, ultimately, turn out to be nonsense when the underlying disorder is not known.

Nova continued: "Kraft has a sister in Atlantic City, only a few blocks from here. I'll go see her in the morning. Now let's deal with you. Does anyone know you're here?"

"No. Not really." Of course Mrs. Tunney knew, but that could be discounted.

"But you're scared anyway. Right?"

"Don't you think I should be?"

"Hard to tell. Anyway, there's not enough for me to get an order of protection for you."

"Do you think I'm acting like a child, Detective Nova? Or that I'm just a coward? Believe me, a vet can't exist without physical courage. Did you ever try to walk into a stall to give a sedative to a crazed stallion who stands almost seventeen hands high?"

"Calm down, Doctor."

Didi was too agitated to sit. She scooped up her visitor's sandwich bag, crumpled it violently, and flung it into the small trash can.

"Look, Dr. Nightingale, why don't you stay here for the night. Then, tomorrow, we'll see. I'll come by in the morning. Does that make sense?"

Didi had no idea what made sense. She nodded yes, anyway. Craig Nova walked out. She immediately dropped into the lotus position and began intense breathing exercises.

Charlie Gravis thought the object by the side of the road was a deer—a wounded deer hit by a vehicle.

He pulled Trent Tucker's pickup truck onto the shoulder and got out. It was very dark. He took one, two, three steps toward the rumpled object and pulled up short.

Sure, he was a bit hearing-impaired, but there was no doubt that wounded deer was singing, or humming.

Maybe, Charlie thought, it's a primal death gurgle.

The deer sprang at him. Charlie tried to run back to the truck, but he moved too slowly. The deer bolted past him, then stood between him and the vehicle, blocking any further progress.

Charlie was now not only confused but astounded, because the deer began to laugh.

Astonishment turned to anger. It wasn't a deer at all, just an inebriated old poet. The famous rural poet, Burt Conyers. Poet or village idiot. One and the same. There he was in his sheepskin vest, sandals, and staff.

Five years ago, a PBS station had done a piece on Conyers, portraying him as a kind of eccentric Robert Frost composing verse about eros and death and resurrection . . . in dairy country. A few tourists and professors still sought him out. But for natives of Hillsbrook, he was a cross to bear. He lived nowhere and everywhere, in all seasons.

It was rumored that he was so broke he satisfied his addiction to alcohol with gasoline filtered through stale black bread and cut with cranberry juice.

"Whither do you go, Charles?" he demanded hoarsely. One could never tell whether Burt was drunk—or how drunk.

"To Ike Badian's," Charlie said.

"I'll come along. Yes, I shall. Did you ever read my poem 'Badian's Lament in the Derelict Orchard'?"

"No, I missed that one. But climb on in, if you're coming."

They drove the few miles out to Badian's farm. Ike was waiting in the near-empty barn. Its silence made Charlie's heart sink. Only four cows left.

"Where did you pick *him* up?" Ike said to Charlie.

"On the road."

Badian took out a cigar and a book of matches and handed them to the poet. "Just sit there and smoke and keep your mouth shut. And watch where you're dumping the ash. Use that old peach can."

Tall, gaunt Burt Conyers took the gift, bowed, and said, "You have the exquisite manners of a large-mouth bass."

"Let's get to work," Charlie said.

"You know, Charlie, I've been thinking," said Ike. "In that bar, your idea seemed OK. But now, as I've been thinking, I got a bad feeling it's just another one of your disastrous schemes."

"No, Ike! No! No! No! This one is paydirt. Believe me. It's too simple to fail. It's the right time at the right place with the right food."

"But, Charlie, we can't cook."

"I'll get to that in a minute. But first, the name."

"Name of what?"

"The restaurant's name. I've been doing some reading. The really 'in' restaurants downstate don't even put up the name on the door. Nothing. We'll do the same. But for technical purposes we'll call it Ike's Place. OK?"

"Not bad."

"Nothing inside the barn is touched—get it? We just bring in ten big old tables . . . maybe from that thrift store on Route 44. And forty-some-odd chairs. Any kind. Four chairs to a table. The cows stay just where they are. You get the picture? Authentic. The more the cows carry on, the better. Authentic farm dining."

"Charlie, there's no kitchen in this barn."

"So what? We cook in your house and carry the food to the barn. Maybe we get a cart."

There was silence. The two conspiratorial entrepreneurs digested the scenario. Ike chewed his cigar thoughtfully.

Finally he said, "OK, Charlie, what you say is fine. Now let's get back to the original problem. You and me ain't cooks."

"Anybody can cook, dammit, Ike. All you need is a recipe."

"Ah, you mean we steal the menu from that place in town and then find the recipes for the same dishes they serve."

"No! Not that. We need a particular cuisine. We need our own unique menu. Like I said, it has to be a resurrection of something lost. Get it? We have to offer dozens of authentic dishes from the area that were lost for fifty, a hundred, a hundred and fifty years."

"Name one."

Charlie did not reply.

"I'm waiting."

"Well," Gravis explained, "some research is necessary."

"Nonsense!"

It was Burt Conyers who had shouted the word. He walked up to Charlie and poked him in the chest. "You are looking at an extraordinary chef. I am the man who codified and refined Hudson Hobo cuisine. The recipes are all in my head and in my heart."

Ike spat. "What the hell is Hudson Hobo cuisine?"

"The dishes of the migrant farm workers as they moved up and down the Hudson River Valley. My good friends, weren't you aware that nouvelle cuisine comes from the campfires of the Hudson hoboes? At least, tangentially."

Ike turned to Charlie, perplexed. "What the hell is he talking about?"

Gravis ignored him and spoke directly to the poet: "We're looking for lost farm recipes. Not farm workers' recipes. Or hoboes'."

"Six of one . . . half dozen of another. It was a time of brilliant synthesis of land and river, of forest and dairy barn—of English, Dutch, Irish, Huron, Negro, and Samoan."

"*Samoan!*" Ike yelled incredulously. "Charlie, get this idiot out of my barn!"

"No, wait, Ike. Just wait. OK, Burt, give me one recipe."

The poet smiled and planted his staff. "And how shall I be recompensed?"

"You got a bottle in the house?" Charlie asked Ike.

"Yeah. Jim Beam."

"Bring it."

An unhappy Ike Badian went into the house and came back with the bottle. He handed it to Charlie, who unscrewed the cap.

"One swig, one recipe, Burt."

"Two swigs, one recipe," the poet countered.

"Deal." Charlie handed the bottle over. Conyers dropped his staff and cradled the bottle like a young lamb. He took one long drink, then rested, happy.

Raising the bottle again, he took another long deep swallow, then handed the bottle back to Charlie.

But before he could recite the recipe, he collapsed, hitting the ground and rolling over. He was babbling something, gurgling.

The other two propped him up against a barn wall.

"He can't handle good whiskey," Badian diagnosed in disgust.

"Keep him here, Ike. I'll be back tomorrow. He owes us."

Chapter 7

Dr. Nightingale opened the motel room door a slit. It was just past nine in the morning. A chilly gray morning.

Detective Craig Nova was standing in the hallway holding two containers of coffee.

"Well?" he asked slyly.

"Well, what?" The day was just beginning, but Didi was already a bit testy.

"Any assaults? Break-ins? Any kind of mayhem whatsoever?"

Not bothering to answer, she swung the door open. Nova walked inside, handing her one of the containers. Then he produced a buttered roll—cut in half, he announced, so that they could share it.

While they were eating and talking about the most mundane subject imaginable, the weather,

Didi made the decision to tell him about the tethered lamb on the embankment.

He listened impassively, then said, "I don't know what to make of that."

She went on to tell him about the relative nonexistence of Ann Huggins, a fact she had not omitted on purpose but had simply forgotten to recount.

This energized him. "Strange," he said. "She gave us an address and telephone number in Toronto when we questioned her in the shoe store."

He went immediately to the phone and called the homicide unit in the state trooper barracks. He got the Toronto number and called it.

"A fake number," he said, putting down the receiver.

"It's like a computerized traffic grid," Didi remarked.

"What do you mean?"

"Lights flashing all over the Eastern Seaboard and Canada. Accidents. Murders. Vanishings. In North Philadelphia. In Hillsbrook. In Cape May. In Toronto. Florida. Atlantic City."

"You have a point, Dr. Nightingale."

"Have you ever used your weapon, Detective?" she asked suddenly, not knowing why she'd posed the question, but profoundly curious.

"Twice. But before I made detective."

"Did you kill a man?"

"Kill? No. A woman was wounded by me in a gunfight on the Jersey Turnpike, just north of Camden. She was in a van, part of a team bringing contraband weapons up from Georgia. Why do you ask?"

"No reason."

"Look, why don't you come with me to see Kraft's sister. You were the one who met her brother."

"Fine."

They walked six blocks to a dreary attached brick house with a porch. It was filled with relatives and friends of the deceased.

Celia Kraft was a woman of about fifty, dressed in black with no jewelry or makeup. She looked enough like her dead brother to be his twin. But then Didi realized that the woman was younger. She was seated on a straight-backed mahogany chair in the center of the living room, ignoring the murmured condolences of her many visitors.

Nova introduced himself and Didi. Celia Kraft ignored Didi and addressed the cop: "Have you found the madman who did this to Milo?"

"I'm not handling the investigation, Ms. Kraft.

I'm a New Jersey State Trooper. Your brother was murdered in North Philadelphia."

"Then why are you here? I told the police everything I know last night."

"His car."

"What about it?"

"He visited my companion here two days ago at her home. He drove up to Dutchess County to see her, in his own car. Then he got on an Amtrak train to come south. Why would he do that? Had his car broken down? Did he call you about it? Did you know he was on that train?"

"I don't know anything about his car. I don't know why he was on the train either."

Talking seemed to hurt the woman. Her body was clinching, then relaxing, then clinching again. As if the alphabet were twenty-six kinds of weapons.

"Mrs. Kraft, I have just a few more simple questions. Your brother claimed he was in Hillsbrook investigating the murder of a veterinarian named Eleazar Wynn. Were you aware of that?"

"No. I didn't know where he was or what he was doing. He just told me he'd be away for a few days."

"Do you know if your brother was working as a private investigator?"

"He was retired. He didn't work anymore."

"Did he ever speak to you about the murder of Lucien Hanratty? He was one of your brother's informers."

"Harmony," Didi corrected.

"Of course," Celia Kraft said. "But Lucien was Milo's friend, not an informer."

"Was there—"

She cut Nova off midsentence. "Go away now. Take your friend with you. Do you hear me? Leave!"

As they walked out she began to scream: "Send flowers! Send flowers!"

Was it sarcasm?

As the door closed behind them, Didi caught a last glimpse of Celia Kraft. The woman looked exactly as she had when they had entered: quiet and calm in her dowdy mourning clothes.

Shock, Didi thought, the woman was sliding in and out of shock.

"Let's take a walk," Detective Nova suggested, striding out. Didi fell into step beside him.

"What I don't understand," she said, "is why Milo Kraft told me Lucien Harmony was a police informant. His sister really seemed to take offense at that characterization. She called him a friend. Why would the brother lie to me?"

"I don't know."

"Where are we going?"

"I have to get out of here and do some work. But the bar where Harmony got iced is close by. I figure we should take a look."

"A bar? It's only ten in the morning."

"Yeah, but the Green Pastures, I hear, opens for breakfast."

The bar called Green Pastures was just off the main shopping street in downtown Atlantic City. It was not an area frequented by the casino people.

The outside of the bar reminded Didi of Irish pubs she had seen in New York City and Albany—festooned with shamrocks and blinking neon signs advertising various beers and ales.

Inside, however, the bar was dark and cavernous with nothing on the walls but two deer trophy heads, undersized at that.

She was astonished at the number of men and women drinking there at that hour of the morning.

The booths were empty and Craig Nova ushered her into the one closest to the door.

"Do you want anything to drink, Dr. Nightingale?"

"No."

They sat there, totally ignored by the drinkers and the bartender. It was strange how quiet the place was.

"Right here is where it happened," Nova announced.

"In this booth?"

"Right where you're sitting."

Didi leaned back. She realized that there was music playing in the bar, very low, someone singing "The Man I Love." It wasn't coming from the jukebox—maybe a radio or a tape deck.

"An uncanny coincidence, wouldn't you say, Dr. Nightingale? Harmony and Wynn were murdered by the same kind of weapon in the same way. They were both seated near a door. Someone they knew well walked in, approached without anyone else in the place noticing. No one heard anything either. And then . . . *wham!* Yet the third murder, while it involved the same kind of weapon, did not otherwise resemble the other two murders."

"Did the Atlantic City police ever identity any suspects in the Harmony murder?"

"No. At least not according to the case file. But if this Milo Kraft was still working the case after he retired—who knows?"

Didi speculated: "I agree. Everything seems to point to one individual who knew and murdered all three for reasons unknown. But how does one find such an individual? I mean, you would have to compile an exhaustive biography of each of the victims and then find one person who is in each of the biographies."

"Exactly. Impossible to do," Nova agreed, "particularly when several jurisdictions are involved. Our only shot is to find the source of those letter openers."

They sat in silence for a while.

"I have to go," Nova said, but made no move. "Tell me about the murderer, Doctor."

She laughed nervously. "What do you mean?"

"I mean, do you think he is a vet, or a physician?"

"Why would I think that?"

"The assault . . . all three assaults . . . were almost surgical. The weapon was driven into the neck in the exact spot where it could cause the most damage in the shortest time."

"Oh, look, a child can find that artery in the neck just by looking at a high school textbook on anatomy."

"I guess you're right," he said, smiling. "You know, I have the funniest feeling that you are not telling me everything you know."

"Why would I withhold information?"

"I don't know."

They got up and left the bar.

"Let's keep in touch," Nova said, "and let's keep vigilant."

"By all means," she agreed. Nova walked away.

The sun had broken through. A breeze kicked up. She could smell saltwater taffy. She walked toward the water, reaching it just at the point where the ocean formed a small bay.

She stopped and looked—a stunning vista with ocean, bay, boardwalk, and the casinos lined up like toy soldiers.

Didi became very calm. Her fear was dissolving. She watched the gulls flying raucously and low along the shore, zooming over the boats anchored in the bay marina.

Suddenly her eyes focused on the boat in the third slip from the beginning of the dock. It was not a sailboat like most of the others. It was a motor yacht, and a grand one, with a high second deck, the prow rising sleekly out of the water.

Why did it fix her gaze? She was baffled at first, but the most uncomplicated of all reasons quickly emerged.

She had seen the boat before. In the photo that Joy Wynn had shown her in Hillsbrook.

It was the boat that formed the backdrop for the group portrait of the top management of the Mid-Florida Equine Clinic.

Why was the yacht still in the marina? The convention was over. The vet was dead.

Were they simply leaving the boat in the marina until the other arrangements, whatever they were, could be made?

Was someone being sent to take the boat south? That was a believable enough explanation.

She approached along the dock, then switched direction when she realized it was of little significance why the boat was still there.

At that precise moment, as she turned, she saw the outline—or was it a shadow?—of two people in a window on the lower deck.

She walked swiftly over to the boat and leaned over from dockside so that her hands were resting on the yacht's railing.

What she witnessed was startling.

Not only had two of the people from the photograph come to life, so to speak, and appeared in the window—they were now clawing at each other's clothing. Not with hatred, with desire. This was sex . . . eros . . . passion.

Embarrassed by her voyeurism, Didi literally slinked away.

When she reached the end of the dock, a strong breeze from the ocean whipped across her face. God, it smelled good.

She stopped and threw her head back so she could catch all of it. The breeze kept swirling. It made her lightheaded, almost giddy. The smell of sea water became stronger—a pungent elixir.

She realized she shouldn't leave the dock area yet. She had a chance to confirm or deny her fears.

She had never met those two people on the yacht. They were known to her only from the photograph that Joy Wynn had flashed before her eyes so briefly in Hillsbrook.

But what if *they* knew *her*?

If they knew her, it might well mean her fears were valid—she was indeed being stalked by wolves.

If they didn't know her face, it might well mean that she was just a random input, irrelevant to past and future murders.

It would be wise, she thought, to confront one or both as they left the shipboard orgy.

But when would they leave? In five minutes or five hours?

She would wait for a while, she decided.

She leaned against a small locked shed on which was written PROPERTY OF HARBORMASTER. NO TRESPASSING.

It took almost an hour for a figure to walk off the boat and down the dockside.

The woman was walking slowly. A short, thin, almost olive-complexioned young woman with long, jet black hair. She was wearing a short rain slicker, black jeans, and light blue running shoes.

It was obvious she was humming a tune. It was obvious from the tune and the smile on her face and her slow, luxuriating stroll that she was happy; that the sex had been good; that she was savoring the memory of it.

Didi felt a twinge of contempt. She didn't like people who were happy after sex, although she sometimes was. And she didn't like people who were sad after sex—more common—although she had many times experienced profound post-coital depression.

Dr. Nightingale had come to believe that, in at least this one area of existence, the nonhuman animals were vastly superior to humans.

Didi had assisted in all kinds of breeding operations—stallions, bulls, boars—and she had supervised dozens of carefully orchestrated matings in the canine world.

Always, she had been struck by the remarkable uniformity of response by animals after coitus.

The were not sad. They were not happy. They were not tired. They were not hyper.

They would remain still, very still, and just gaze out at the scenery, or at nothing.

Dr. Nightingale had tried to mimic that animal stance after making love with Allie, but she could never pull it off.

As the young woman approached, Didi could see that while she was thin, she was strongly built, wiry, sinewy—as befitted someone who worked with fractious Thoroughbred horses.

Dr. Nightingale had seen seventeen-year-old racetrack girls who didn't weigh more than 105 pounds fling around bales of hay as if they were heads of lettuce.

Didi stepped away from the shed and blocked the young woman's path. She saw a flicker of fear in her eyes.

"I didn't mean to startle you," Didi said, "but I'm a bit lost."

The stranger recovered and made a happy little quip: "Everyone is lost in Atlantic City." Then she asked: "Where do you want to go?"

"The Convention Center."

The young woman nodded and pointed. "There's the boardwalk. Just follow it. You can't miss the center. It's *on* the boardwalk."

Didi didn't respond. They were staring at each other now. Didi saw no glint of recognition, but the young woman's voice had become utterly flat. She sounded suddenly like someone who would never hum again, no matter how good and wild the sex.

Dr. Nightingale became confused. The girl seemed to have no idea who she was. Perhaps. This girl was strange, unreadable.

"Maybe," she said, "you really don't want to go to the Convention Center."

"Why would I ask you directions to a place if I didn't want to go to that place?" Didi snapped at her.

The young woman smiled and walked on. Didi felt like a fool, not one whit wiser about anything.

Rose stood outside the back door of her barn and contemplated the contours of her land. She was searching for the best place to plant a vegetable garden.

She had made such a survey every year since she had moved from Manhattan to Hillsbrook, and had never managed to put in a garden.

Rose could never really understand her procrastination in regard to this task, but she had an inkling that it was connected to a disquiet with the life she had chosen. No, not a reversal of her back-to-nature philosophy, but a growing realization that she had picked the wrong place to go "back" to.

Hillsbrook was not a rural utopia. In fact, it was no longer even rural. Just a suburb with a few woods, a whole lot of deer, a few cows, and a great many eccentrics with money playing the game of gentleman farmer.

Her dogs, who had been snoozing in the sun, suddenly let out a corporate yelp and bolted toward the front of the barn. Rose shouted at them. They ignored her as usual. She followed them to the front and saw their prey: Albert Voegler getting out of his unmarked police vehicle.

They jumped all over him in a kindly fashion. He was carrying packages.

"I have some things for you," he said in a quiet voice.

"This isn't Christmastime and you're not Santa Claus."

The dogs let up on their friendly assault and flopped down—except for Huck, the corgi, who ran over the young shepherd Bozo to get to the front wheel of Voegler's car, against which he raised his leg.

"I didn't bring frivolous gifts. They're for survival," he explained.

"Why should you bring me any gifts at all?"

"I'm quirky," he replied, and handed her a bag of tortilla chips—a very large bag.

"In other words," he continued, "I'm saying that I don't really make judgments about the way people live."

"Chips are not a way of life," she said, but took the bag.

"I have something else for you. Do you have a rug or a mat I can use?"

She led him into the barn, where he selected one of the many straw mats and immediately got on his knees and began to empty the large container. The contents he spilled out seemed to add up to a heap of metal.

"Well, there it is . . . and it's all yours."

Rose fell to her knees on the mat, across the pile of scrap.

"What am I supposed to do with it?" she asked. The dogs were already investigating.

"Assemble it. It's an old but fine .22 caliber rifle. For those rats by the water pipe."

Rose exhaled. She had fired a rifle before, but she had never seen one disassembled. She felt stupid. The barrel and the trigger housing were easy to spot even in the disassembled state.

"Whose is it?" she asked.

"Yours, now. It used to be mine, but I haven't used it in years. Old but good, believe me. Now watch!"

Voegler proceeded to assemble the weapon slowly, naming each part as he placed it in sequence.

When the weapon was fully assembled on the

mat, he leaned back and stared at Rose. She stared back. It was an odd, silent exchange. She felt he was identifying her as someone who could be violent. Someone, perhaps, who could kill a man as well as a water rat.

Then he leaned over and broke the rifle down again, pushing the pieces close to her.

"Now you do it," he said.

She assembled it painstakingly, making many errors along the way, but always able to figure out where she had gone wrong.

She held the weapon up triumphantly.

"Good job!" He took a box of cartridges from his pocket and handed her one bullet at a time.

"Load them through the slot on the side. Slowly. It holds eight."

She accomplished that.

"Now lever it once."

She worked the lever.

"There you are, Rose. A round is in the chamber. The weapon is now loaded. Put on the safety."

She put the safety lock on.

"Do you like the way it feels?"

"Yes."

"It's a fine weapon."

"Thank you. Would you like a cup of tea?"

"Sure."

They both got off the mat. She headed for the wood-burning stove, still holding the light weapon by the stock.

"Let me hold it," he suggested. She thrust the weapon out, barrel first. He took it and leaned it against a wall. She busied herself with the boiling of water. She heard him playing with the dogs.

Then she sensed that he was coming very close to her. Too close.

She whirled. He was inches away. His flannel shirt smelled damp but beautiful. Like the bark of a pear tree.

He whispered: "Don't you understand, Rose? She abandoned both of us. She brought us together."

He put his hands on her waist. He kissed her softly on the lips.

She kissed him back, fiercely. She was going to make love with this man, she knew. She didn't know why.

Dr. Nightingale sat on a deep-cushioned chair in the opulent lobby of the casino across the street from her motel.

She was still uneasy. The sex scene she had witnessed on the boat was bizarre. It was "movie" sex, unreal . . . grown people in midmorning flailing at each other in a riot of lust. Didi had always found movie sex extremely stupid. That was never the way it really happened. It was like the Hollywood view of veterinarians.

Her brief conversation with the young woman had been absurd. And it had resolved nothing.

The sounds in the casino were perplexing at first, like flocks of birds opening pumpkin seeds. The slot machines, she realized. Of course, it was the slots.

It took her a while to remember the names of those passionate people—Joy Wynn had mentioned them only once when she presented the photo.

But remember them Didi did.

Dr. Arthur Bremen, Eleazar Wynn's partner.

And Mary Alonso, foreman of the Mid-Florida Equine Clinic.

Once having remembered them—at least their faces as they appeared in the photo and their names as Joy Wynn had spoken them—she realized the recollection didn't mean a damn thing to her.

She walked out of the casino and back to her motel room. It had been a very long morning. She sat down on the side of the bed, then stretched out.

Suddenly she wanted fiercely to speak to

someone she knew, someone from home. Should she tell Charlie Gravis? Maybe Rose Vigdor. Maybe Mrs. Tunney.

Didi made no call. She laughed at herself, thinking: Have I become a little rich girl again, crying for home and Mommy?

Didi looked at the chair. On it was the open attaché case with the manuscript. The maid had obviously moved it from the bed to the chair when she changed the sheets.

She retrieved the manuscript from the case and brought it back to the bed. Whatever was happening, she was still being paid good money to read the manuscript critically.

For the second time she commenced to read it, determined to take coherent notes right on the relevant pages.

At about page 11 she began to find coffee stains on the pages. Not many and not on all the pages, but enough to make her feel ashamed. She prided herself on not being sloppy.

Then she realized that at no time—either in Hillsbrook or on that aborted train ride or in the motel room—had she ever handled the manuscript while drinking coffee or anything else.

She put the manuscript down quickly and began to scan the room fearfully.

Someone has been in here, she thought. Someone else has been reading this manuscript.

Her eyes searched out the objects she had brought: the clothes, the toilet articles, the suitcase, the attaché case. All seemed intact, unmoved, undisturbed.

Or were they? She tried to remember the exact placement of the objects when she had left in the morning with Craig Nova to visit Celia Kraft.

She picked up the manuscript again and leafed through the pages. The stains loomed larger and larger in her psyche . . . as if they had been placed there purposefully by an intruder . . . as if that intruder had left a coded message in the stains.

A message to whom? For what? Why coffee?

She laughed out loud. I am losing all my marbles, she thought.

After the recovery and interrogation of Burt Conyers, and after the poet had staggered off into the woods with the gift bottle, the two old dairy farmers left the barn and repaired to Ike Badian's immense but gloomy kitchen in the main house.

Then, seated at the table covered with linoleum cloth, they reconstructed the dishes the poet had revealed, the ones that were, in his words, the "signature" dishes . . . the glory of the long-lost Hudson Hobo cuisine.

Charlie did the actual writing, on the backs of Ike's unpaid telephone bills.

As he wrote, Ike protested: "This is getting crazier and crazier, Charlie. He only gave us three dishes. And he didn't really give us recipes for each one. Just hints. Besides, who's going to eat that slop? Worse—what kind of idiots would pay good money to taste it?"

Charlie ignored him.

Ike got louder. "Listen, Charlie! How can we open a restaurant serving only three things? And three mains at that? What about soup and salad and dessert?"

Charlie waved his objections off as if they were too trivial to dignify with an answer. He kept on working.

Five minutes later he was finished.

"We have them!" he announced triumphantly and proceeded to lay out the menu.

"First we have spaghetti and woodchuck. No problem there. Except for the sauce. The poet didn't give us one but we'll improvise. Let's call it Dutchess Farm Pasta. And we'll call the woodchuck 'young boar.' The second dish is Wild Turkey Chili. No problem there, either. We'll call it Mrs. Warren's Chili."

"Wait!" Ike interrupted. "Who's Mrs. Warren?"

"I don't know. Don't bother me with nonsense,

Ike. Let's keep focused. The third dish is a problem. Burt said it was diced apples with stray dog or cat. Here we better make a substitution. What about cow brains? That's a gourmet dish in Europe, right? So, it'll be apple and cow brains. Let's call it Harvest Quiche. It ain't technically a quiche, but what the hell—we'll bake it like chicken pot pie . . . close enough. Remember, Ike, in all these dishes the really beautiful thing is that all the ingredients are authentic. It don't matter what we call it on the menu. We are being historically correct. This is Hudson Hobo cuisine, although of course we have to keep the 'hobo' out of it."

Ike just sat there. He didn't respond. He appeared to be in shock.

"Do you know what our next step is, Ike?"

Wearily, warily, Ike replied, "I haven't the slightest idea."

"We cook the dishes and eat them ourselves. A full dress rehearsal. Get those pots down!"

Charlie jumped out of his chair and bolted from the kitchen.

Ike didn't make a move toward the pots. He just sat there, still in a kind of trance. Things were moving fast; things were getting out of control.

Charlie crashed back in, shouting: "Here, Ike! Take it!"

Badian found himself staring at his own shotgun.

"What am I supposed to do with this, Charlie?"

"Well, you're the manager and assistant chef of Ike's Place. So get me the main ingredients of Dutchess Farm Pasta. And I ain't talking about the spaghetti, if you get my drift."

"Why can't I just be the waiter?" Ike asked forlornly.

It grew dark. Didi had not left the motel room since coming back there midmorning. With the encroaching darkness came the fear again.

Craig Nova called at 6 P.M. He wanted to know what she was doing.

She blurted out what she had seen taking place on the yacht, and her suspicions that someone had entered her room and read Wynn's manuscript. Detective Nova did not seem particularly interested in her revelations.

He had one of his own: "I got a tip on someone who knew Lucien Harmony. Name of Moe Brady. I'm meeting him in the Green Pastures bar in an hour. You want to keep me company?"

Didi hesitated.

What was going on with this detective? Why did he keep seeking out her company for his quixotic inquiries?

Was he just being gallant, to allay her fears? Did he really believe she was in danger? Did he still believe she was withholding information about the Eleazar Wynn murder? Or was it simply that he liked her as a man likes a woman?

Who knew? Didi didn't.

"Fine," she agreed.

"I'll ring your bell in an hour," he said. Didi waited inside until he arrived. She strongly suspected that the intruder who had spilled coffee on the Wynn papers was keeping her under surveillance.

Nova showed up fifteen minutes early. They drove to the bar in his vehicle and met Moe Brady in the same booth they had occupied that very morning, the same booth in which Lucien Harmony had been murdered two years earlier.

Brady was an old black man dressed in a chauffeur's outfit. He had several rings on his fingers. He seemed nervous, jumpy, anxious to be of help.

"How long did you know Harmony, Mr. Brady?" the detective asked.

"Twenty years at least."

"Did you know Milo Kraft?"

"Sure."

"Was Harmony his informer?"

"Not that I know."

"Then what was their relationship?"

"Friends. They drank together."

"Did Lucien Harmony ever mention a man named Eleazar Wynn to you?"

"Don't think so. The name doesn't ring a bell."

"Mary Alonso?"

Didi tensed as Nova mentioned that name. So the detective had taken seriously the sex scene she had witnessed. Or at least considered it strange enough to put the other members of Mid-Florida Equine back in the investigative pot.

In any case Brady answered, "No."

"What about an Arthur Bremen? Ever hear him mentioned?"

He shook his head. "No. Who are those people?"

"Do you have any idea who killed Lucien Harmony, Mr. Brady?"

"No, of course not."

"Or why?"

"No, I don't. He was a sweet guy, believe me."

"Do you have any idea who'd want Milo Kraft dead?"

"No."

"How did Harmony make a living?"

"Horses."

"You mean he was a bookie?"

"No, no, no."

"So he worked at the track—is that it?"

"No. He *bet* on horses. And he won. He always won."

"Yeah? Where did he do his betting?"

"In a casino. In the horse room at Wonderland."

"This Lucien a lady's man?"

"Well, not exactly. He paid for it."

"And Milo?"

"I didn't know him well enough to figure that out."

That was the end of the dialogue. Didi hadn't said a word so far. Moe Brady never even looked at her. Then Nova bought him a rum and Coke. The man drank it down fast and walked out.

"What do you think?" Nova asked her.

"About what?"

"About Harmony being a hotshot gambler. I heard the guy didn't have two dimes to rub together."

"I haven't heard that expression since I was a child," Didi noted.

"You mean 'two dimes'? Well, it tells a story, doesn't it?"

"The problem is—Moe Brady didn't tell us a

story you could use. I mean, he didn't make the connection between Harmony and the Wynns. If he could have, Detective Nova, at least there'd be some kind of logic."

The detective laughed at her speculation.

"Let me tell you something, Madam Vet. At this point, if Brady had told me that Joy Wynn was a hooker and Harmony had paid for services, I still wouldn't have a clue about three murder victims with letter openers sticking out of their necks."

He drove her back to the motel. In the car he asked, "You ever bet on horses, Dr. Nightingale?"

"No."

"But you've been at the racetrack, haven't you?"

"Sure. I've treated Thoroughbreds at racetracks, breeding farms, and lay-up stables."

"And you never bet?"

"I find wagering on horse races ridiculous!"

She began to get irritated with his line of questioning. She continued: "OK. Look at it this way, Detective. At many racetracks beautiful horses are run until they collapse. Then they're put down. It's a bizarre form of slavery. Now do you understand why I don't bet on horses? I want to make hurt animals well; I don't want to help destroy them."

He chuckled at her explosion. The way he laughed made her think of Allie Voegler.

There was no further discussion. He dropped her in front of the motel, then drove off. Didi looked around furtively. If the manuscript voyeur was following her, he or she was doing it expertly.

She didn't want to go into her room. She walked to the corner, up the ramp, and onto the boardwalk. The ocean breeze was heady and sweet.

What is it with men like Nova and Allie? she thought.

What is it with women like me who get involved with them?

She had nothing in common with either of them; however, she had been Allie's lover and she was now essentially assisting Nova in a criminal investigation.

They were violent men, on the right side of the law, of course, but still violent. Their world was a macho one—hunting, gambling, and God knows what else. They craved any kind of power they could get.

She was a healer. She lived to stop pain and death and degradation in the creatures she loved.

Didi walked to the railing and leaned over.

The beach was lovely, the sand like a closely woven carpet.

She turned and leaned her back against the railing, staring down the boardwalk.

Her eyes fixed on one particular casino marquee blinking ferociously in the night—Wonderland.

Wonderland? That was the place where Lucien Harmony had gambled—in the horse room.

Horse rooms. Didi had heard of them. Places in the casino set aside for wagering on horses, filled with all kinds of high-tech video systems and betting machines. She had never been in one.

She kept staring at the sign. Maybe she should visit one. Maybe she should even gamble a bit. After all, she had plenty of cash and traveler's checks now.

Maybe she should spend a few nights in one of the hotel rooms to really see what the male animal was all about. That way, she wouldn't make any more mistakes in regard to men.

She started to laugh at the absurdity of her plan. Then the laughter died. She was alone. It might be over with Allie Voegler, but she missed him in a hundred ways, even down to their coffee and donut dates together. That was always the way it had been with Allie and her. Sometimes she never gave a thought to him. Sometimes she became obsessed with him.

She headed toward the ramp to return to the motel.

Suddenly, inexplicably, she thought of that tethered lamb on the embankment. It still meant nothing to her, but she had the strange feeling that if she returned to the motel, she would find such a little white creature tethered somewhere in the room.

Not pleasant. Little white lambs now meant a corpse somewhere.

She stopped.

Where do I go now?

Why not the Wonderland? Why not have a drink there and watch the boys play and watch the horses run?

As much as she loathed the racing industry, she loved the sight of a two-year-old filly racing toward the wire.

And she knew that it was one of the ironies of life that if one wanted to see a glorious sight such as that, at night, one could only see it in a casino horse-betting room on a wide-screen color television.

She walked quickly down the boardwalk and into the Wonderland. Didi felt a bit wild, a bit out of control. Like the night during her second year at veterinary school when she decided to lose her virginity to a professor.

As she negotiated the revolving doors, she giggled—wondering what her elves would think if they could see her now. That there was a cascade of corpses dropping around Miss Quinn wouldn't surprise them in the least. But their young boss blithely walking into a casino? That they would find incredible.

The horse room was not exactly what she had expected. It was tucked away on the second floor of the casino. The room contained twenty or so tables surrounded by upholstered chairs; tellers' windows; dozens of large television screens implanted in all the walls; and several automated machines for bettors who did not wish any human contact with the tellers.

A Sinatra record was playing very low in the background. Only about thirty or so men and a sprinkling of women inhabited the room. Most stood in front of one TV screen or another.

Three very good-looking young women were serving drinks.

Didi sat down at a table on the periphery. She ordered a Bloody Mary and looked carefully at the screen.

Each one highlighted a single track—either Thoroughbred (flats) or Standardbreed (trots).

Because of the hour and the time differential, most of the flat racing came from the West Coast.

There was even wagering offered from Australian tracks, where the horses ran counter-clockwise.

The drink arrived. She sipped it. So this was where Lucien Harmony had spent his evenings. So what?

On the screen closest to her were the odds for the fifth race at a New Mexico quarter-horse track called Diablo. These kinds of races were fast, short sprints; the horses much more powerfully built and more "gathered" than Thoroughbreds.

Didi smiled. The number 3 horse on the screen was listed at odds of 15–1. His name was Charlie.

She wondered what her Charlie was doing now; probably being harassed by old Mrs. Tunney. Well, Charlie, she thought, this one's for you. She reached into her purse, found her wallet and pulled out a hundred-dollar bill, then walked to a window and told the teller: "Fifty to win and fifty to place on the three horse in the fifth race at Diablo."

She held the ticket gingerly as she walked back to the table. Now I am in their world, she thought, waiting for the kick . . . the charge. It didn't come.

She watched Charlie run. The homely little gelding with funny ears finished with a furious race to place second. He paid twenty dollars for every two-dollar bet placed on him.

That meant her fifty-dollar-place ticket was worth five hundred. She went to the window and cashed it, then returned to her table. Still the kick did not arrive.

Other races at other tracks were going off. Some of the patrons began to shout support for their horses. The mood of the room changed. It became raucous, loathsome.

She regretted her decision to come here. She started to leave.

Suddenly she saw a vaguely familiar face three tables from hers.

He was a young Asian man sitting alone watching one of the screens, calmly tapping the fingers of his right hand on top of the table, as if he were keeping time with a tune in his head.

Bizarre! It was one of the clerks from that shoe store in Cape May. There was no doubt about it.

What was his name? It had been mentioned to her once or twice during the preliminary investigation. Wu. That was the last name. Wu. First name, John—or was it Jack? One of those.

Sad, she thought. He works all day in a shoe

store to earn money to lose at night in the horse room.

But he didn't seem to be gambling, just sitting there quietly, watching, drumming those fingers.

She wanted badly to leave, but still she hesitated. The young man fascinated her. As unlikely as it seemed—although they had shared the gruesome experience of being present at a murder scene—they had never spoken a word to each other.

She went on studying him. Maybe he just came there to relax, to drink, to reflect. Maybe he was a voyeur, like her. But at least she had made one bet, and won.

The irony of the situation did not escape her. Didi was watching the shoe clerk, while someone else—her coffee-drinking intruder—might be watching her. And neither she nor the clerk was guilty of anything. The difference was, he wasn't being hunted; he was in no danger.

She ordered a second Bloody Mary. When the drink arrived, she noticed the young man pull a piece of paper from his pocket, study it, then go to one of the automated betting machines. He came back to the table and resumed his pose, including the drumming.

Ten minutes passed. Didi didn't know whether he'd won or lost. Another ten minutes went by and he repeated the procedure. Didi turned her attention to another table where a middle-aged woman was berating a slightly inebriated man. She was leveling her charges, whatever they were, in a hoarse, vitriolic whisper. He listened, eyes closed, rocking gently in his seat.

She looked at Wu again. He was drumming his fingers and had a faraway look in his eyes. Like the gaze of a postcoital animal. Didi squirmed.

Why was she so reticent? Why didn't she just walk up to him and speak? What kind of investigation was she running? Was it an investigation? Or had she turned into a crumbling, weepy, pathetic hostage?

Could he hurt her? Hardly. Was he involved? A very long shot. He was her comrade in the horror. He had been in that shoe store with her. He must know something. Fate had put him, also, in the wrong place at the wrong time.

She left her drink and walked to his table.

"Hello!" she said, with a bit too much bravura.

He looked up at her, still drumming his fingers on the table. He was quite a handsome young man, she realized, and his present clothing was totally different from his shoe store garb. He was wearing a tailored gray suit with a black turtleneck. His black hair was brilliantly brushed back, parted in the middle.

Like a Hong Kong gangster, Didi thought. Or one of the Taiwanese literati.

He was looking at her as if she was soliciting drinks.

"Do you know who I am?" she asked.

His face lit up.

"Ah, yes! You were in the store that afternoon."

"That's right, I was." But she realized she no longer remembered exactly whether the shoe store murder had occurred in the morning, afternoon, or evening.

"Do you still work there?"

"Sure. Six days in the store. Seven nights here," he replied, then added, "Only the well-balanced life is worth living."

Of course he's being sarcastic, she thought. But she couldn't be sure. She waited for him to ask her to sit down. He didn't.

"Have there been any further repercussions?" she asked.

"I don't know what you're talking about."

"I'm talking about the murder of Eleazar Wynn."

"What kind of repercussions do you mean?"

"Oh, you know. Anything."

"The cops spoke to me one more time. That's all."

"Did you ever meet the murdered man's wife?"

"No," he replied, and his eyes seemed to be pulled toward the overhead screens, where two races were now in progress. It was obvious he wanted to get on with his gambling.

"Do you win often?"

"Often enough. Hell, I have a town house and a Land Rover. I couldn't survive on a shoe store job."

"I used to know a very good gambler," Didi lied. "His name was Lucien Harmony. Did you know him, by any chance?"

"Never heard the name."

"And I knew a bad gambler. A man who lost everything. Milo Kraft. You know him?"

"No. Do you play the horses?"

"My first time tonight. I made one bet and won some money."

"Maybe you have the touch."

"What touch?"

"Picking winners."

"Maybe I do. Look, I don't mean to be intrusive, but did you ever see that woman again?"

"What woman?"

"The other woman in the shoe store. She was tall—very tall. We came in together."

"No."

"Well, it was good seeing you again," Didi said. She turned and headed back toward her table.

"Hold it."

She turned back. He was smiling broadly and drumming furiously. "If you get another tip, pass it along—OK? I can use all the veterinary help I can get." And then he laughed.

She felt deflated. She walked back to her table and sat down. What to do next?

As she turned the key in the lock, she realized how sleepy she was—and how grateful she should be to her ludicrous gambling adventure for helping her achieve that blessed state.

But the moment she got inside and locked the door behind her, sleep went on the back burner. She smelled whiskey, a very heavy dose of it, like a blanket on the air.

She flicked on the light and was so startled by what she saw that she stepped back instinctively, rapping her head against the closed door.

A man was lying on her bed.

"Get out!" she yelled, thinking for a moment it was Allie Voegler.

But he wasn't Allie and he wasn't drunk—or at least no longer just drunk.

He was also dead.

One side of his head had been bashed in. The base of the phone next to the bed was drenched in blood.

And knotted around his neck was a sweater she had brought with her: a lovely brown merino wool cardigan.

"You are the man in the yacht window," she accused the dead figure crazily. And then she slid down the door until she reached the floor.

It was twenty minutes before she had the strength to notify the motel manager. Her phone was no longer operative.

Albert Voegler sat alone in a tavern a few miles outside of Hillsbrook on Route 44.

He had chosen this out-of-the-way pub deliberately. No chance of being seen by anyone who knew him. He had sworn to avoid all alcoholic beverages as part of his reinstatement agreement with the Hillsbrook Police Department.

Drinking this beer wasn't the only crime he had committed.

He had also performed a sexual act while on duty.

He had made love to Didi's best friend.

Three crimes in about as many hours—a helluva performance.

Voegler was not used to being on the wrong side of any law, but he had never felt better in his life.

He drank that first beer very slowly, lip-smacking in an almost vaudevillian manner, savoring every drop. It had been a long time between beers.

When finished, he ordered another beer but let it stand untouched on the bar.

The sex with Rose Vigdor had been wonderful. He had never been so loose, so natural, so passionate, so gentle, so wild, so fulfilled.

Why? He didn't know. Was it love? He doubted it. Was it just a powerful chemistry? Yes, but it was more. And it was odd. For years he had rarely said a friendly word to her—and he had never thought of her sexually.

That situation had changed suddenly in the past few days.

Every time he saw her in town, he needed to speak to her. He needed *her*. And now he knew that she needed him as well.

The whole thing was wonderfully perplexing. He didn't love Rose Vigdor. He loved Didi Nightingale.

But never had the sex with Didi been so good as this one time with Rose.

He took a long swallow from the second beer. He had to be careful, he knew, not to lose control and order whiskey. And he had to keep his eyes open on the chance that someone who could recognize him might walk into the bar.

He wondered what Didi was doing in Florida now.

He wondered if she was thinking of him, asking herself why things had been going badly between them and how they could be righted.

He saw his image in the mirror across the bar. Albert smiled to himself and then was struck with the most peculiar thought of all—maybe even an insight: Was it possible that Didi had set this whole thing up in some way?

Was it possible she wanted him and Rose to become lovers? Did she have a secret agenda that neither he nor Rose could fathom? It was possible.

He held up the beer bottle and spoke to it: "I am thinking like a cop."

Chapter 8

Mrs. Tunney waited until they were all seated for breakfast and the oatmeal was being ladled out, then she turned loose her venom on Charlie Gravis.

"Do you really think we're fools, Charlie? Do you really think I don't know you got in at two in the morning? You'd better have a very good excuse! Shame on you! A man of your age tomcatting around when Miss Quinn goes away and leaves you in charge. Shame on you!"

All the spoons of all the elves were poised on the cusp of their bowls as they waited for Charlie's answer.

"Professional business," he finally stated, calmly.

"What does that mean?" Mrs. Tunney barked.

"A sick cow."

It was such a blatant lie that no one, not even Mrs. Tunney, had a retort.

The oatmeal fest commenced, amid the passing of sugar and cream.

A few moments into the breakfast, a raucous horn from outside the house began to blow.

Charlie jumped up. "Business calls!" he yelled and left the kitchen abruptly.

"You're playing with fire, you old fool!" Mrs. Tunney shouted after him, a standard warning for everyone, no matter what they were doing.

Charlie Gravis slammed the door shut and climbed into Ike Badian's idling pickup truck.

"I'm exhausted," Ike said.

"So what?"

"So nothing."

The old vehicle chugged off the Nightingale property.

"The table and chairs were delivered this morning," Ike said.

"Good. Now let's find Burt Conyers."

Ike and Charlie had spent hours the previous night cooking the three dishes. The woodchuck came from Ike's shotgun, the turkey from the supermarket, the cow brains from the slaughterer. Everything was ready for the tasting. They had cooked with an innocent, incompetent, desperate fury and produced three huge vats of the delicacies, which now lay safely in Ike's ancient, cavernous freezer.

"Try the back of Agway first," Charlie suggested.

The poet wasn't there, but fifteen minutes later they found him snoozing by the side truck ramp of the post office. They bundled him into the pickup and drove to Ike's farm.

Once in the barn, they set up the ten beat-up wood tables—some round, some square—and placed the thirty-one chairs around them. Several of the chairs had broken rattan backs, but they were serviceable if one sat gingerly.

The four remaining cows in the Badian dairy operation watched calmly, but with great interest, their tails moving in a syncopated chorus. There were one or two bellows.

"It don't look like a restaurant," Ike noted. "It looks a bit primitive."

"No! No! It's perfect. We're aiming for authenticity."

"Amen," said the poet, still a bit hungover.

They left the barn and entered the kitchen of the house. Charlie thrust Burt into a chair.

"Keep him there," he ordered Ike. Then Charlie carved out a small chunk from each of the three pans in the freezer, placed them on one skillet, and shoved it into the oven.

When the food was heated sufficiently, he placed the skillet in front of Burt Conyers.

"Taste it! You're the expert."

"With pleasure," the poet responded. "I will be impartial."

He tasted critically; he chewed thoughtfully.

When he finished, he pushed the skillet away.

"Let me be blunt, gentlemen. You have performed a miracle. You have recreated the heart, soul, and pancreas of a lost people. You will become legends in your own time. You will be on postage stamps."

Charlie let out a whoop of joy.

Ike, more skeptical, asked, "Are you sure, Burt?"

The poet replied with sincerity: "'If this be error and upon me proved—I never writ, nor no man ever loved.'"

"There's no time to waste," Charlie announced. "You, Burt, write out the invitations. Ike, get him some paper. Make them brief but flowery, Burt. Ike's Place will open tonight. This preview will be free to select diners—the upper crust of Hillsbrook. Ike, you deliver them by hand. Meanwhile, I'll get a maitre d'."

"Whoa, Charlie—whoa!" Badian warned. "What do we need one of those for?"

"Gives the place class. I'm thinking of Luis Ragobert."

"You mean the crazy pig farmer? You can't be serious, Charlie."

"He's not crazy, he's mysterious," Charlie corrected angrily. "And he's not just a pig farmer. He's a dedicated and imaginative researcher into the hidden areas of hog husbandry."

"Yes! Yes!" affirmed a suddenly excited Burt Conyers. "He is in the great tradition!"

"What great tradition?" Ike demanded.

"That of the ancient Chinese emperors who demanded whole pig sties be interred with them in their tombs."

"There's no pork on our menu," Badian retorted.

"Meaningless," snapped the poet.

Where am I?

Didi sat up in bed. It was a large bed. The comforter was quite elegant. And she was simply confused.

She looked around. The room was spacious. The morning sun was flooding through six windows.

Ah! She remembered. She was in a suite in the Tower Casino, right across from the motel where she'd found a dead man in her bed.

Someone began to knock persistently on the door. She looked for a robe, realized she had slept fully dressed, slipped into the shoes by the bed, and let the visitor in.

It was Detective Nova. He, she realized, was the one who'd brought her to the room last night after she'd found the body of Arthur Bremen.

"How are you feeling?" he asked.

"OK."

He handed her a container of coffee. They sat down on the large wingback chairs by the windows.

"It's time you got out of Atlantic City, Dr. Nightingale."

"You mean you finally agree that I'm in danger?"

"No. I mean you're in no danger at all anymore. In fact, we don't even have a mystery anymore. All we have is a one-woman assassination squad. And she's on the road out of here."

"You mean Mary Alonso? The one I saw on the yacht with Bremen?"

"Hell no! It's an old friend of ours—Ann Huggins, aka Shoe Store Sally."

Didi put the coffee container down on an end table.

"Are you sure about that?" she asked, skeptical.

"At about nine o'clock last night a couple bribed the motel clerk to use your room for an hour's worth of sex. It was a sentimental thing, they said. They had stayed in that room ten years ago on their wedding night. The man was Arthur Bremen. According to the clerk's description, the woman was Ann Huggins. No doubt about it."

"How do you know she's left Atlantic City?"

"We have good information that she boarded a bus to Roanoke about an hour after the murder. Even more important, that young woman, Mary Alonso, rented a car three hours before the murder, and headed for Florida. Do you understand what's happening now?"

"No."

"Alonso ran. She knew she was being hunted. The killer caught·up with Bremen instead. For some reason, this madwoman Ann Huggins, or whatever her name is, is hell-bent to kill everybody in the management of the Mid-Florida Equine Clinic. She's on her way to Florida to catch up with Joy Wynn and Alonso. We've alerted every law enforcement agency from here to Orlando. They'll get her."

Didi didn't respond for a while. She sipped a little coffee.

"Are you sure you're OK?" he asked.

"How did he die?" she responded.

"Who?"

"The man on my bed."

"We don't know that for sure yet, but it looks like his skull was fractured by the phone. He was finished off probably by strangulation . . . with your sweater."

"It doesn't make sense to me," Didi announced.

"Well, you've had a rough time, Dr. Nightingale."

"Listen. What about Harmony and Kraft? Remember them? They weren't part of Mid-Florida Equine. And Bremen didn't have one of those signature letter openers in his neck like Harmony, Kraft, and Wynn."

Nova laughed. "Maybe she ran out of letter openers."

"Maybe. But what about the Wynn murder? I was in the shoe store. With Ann Huggins. I never saw her anywhere near Eleazer Wynn. He was at the front of the store. We were in back."

"Look! Sure, there are all kinds of gaps, but we'll fill them in when we get her. The main thing is we have the contours of what's happening. The action has headed south. Now why don't you just go on back to Hillsbrook and work on the manuscript up there."

Dr. Nightingale stood up very quickly.

"What's the matter?" he demanded.

"Where is the manuscript?"

"At the motel," said Nova. "I didn't bring any of your stuff here. You can go and pick it up. The only thing we took from that room of yours was the wool sweater."

He leaned over and patted her on the knee. "Go on back to the motel, Doctor. Talk to the manager. He has your things safely locked up. Your room is still off-limits. Get your belongings and go home. It's over. The dragon lady has moved on."

He walked to the door. "You know what would be nice?" he asked.

"What?"

"If the next time you come to Jersey, we go out together. Relax. Have a good meal. Do a little gambling, a little drinking. Maybe just walk up and down the boardwalk." He laughed. "Maybe even hold hands. You know, I'm a very old-fashioned kind of guy."

"I'm aware of that," was all Didi said.

Nova closed the door softly behind him.

She finished the coffee and crumpled the paper cup. The sun had vanished. Would it rain again? She shivered. It's time, she thought. For what? To pick up my marbles. To throw in my cards. To cash in my chips. To take my ball and leave the game. To put my dolls in the trunk. To hang up my tap shoes.

Yes. Yes! It was time to go home.

The day started on a high note for Rose Vigdor. After a large cup of breakfast mint tea with a dash of honey, she bolted out of her barn carrying her stainless steel garden spade, which she had never used before.

She had purchased it years ago at a fancy housewares store in Manhattan's SoHo, during the intense preliminary phase of her conversion to rural life. It was a silly purchase and she had known it even at the time.

The immediate impetus for the purchase was a book she had read—*The Living Garden*, by George Orish. It told the story of one English garden in Kent over a 400-year span—the people, the plants, the bugs, the birds, the soil.

The book had obsessed her, grabbed her in the heart like a terrier grabs a rat. She identified with each gardener—from Thomas Barton, who in 1560 planted tulips and apple trees . . . to his grandson, who added spinach, asparagus, and cauliflower . . . to the owner in 1730, who obtained evening primrose from America . . . to the trained horticulturist, who enhanced the garden with a spectacular camomile lawn when the property became an old-age home, in the 1980s.

Yes, that book had deranged her and she had bought the ridiculous spade, too expensive and too pretty.

Now, years later, she was finally going to use it. As she trudged past the well to begin the garden, she knew full well that her burst of productivity was inextricably tied to Albert Voegler. It was stupid for it to be that way, and embarrassing—but there it was.

When she reached higher ground beyond the well, she drove the spade into the soil, picked up a handful of stones, and began to lay out the garden using the stones as markers.

Her dogs, who had been prepared for a long walk in the woods, retreated to the edge of the property and watched her labor, confused.

Rose marked out a modest rectangle for her garden. About twenty feet wide and fifty feet long.

Then she retrieved the spade and began to turn over the good soil covered with errant grass and weeds.

Rose Vigdor was a large young woman and she worked with great fervor.

She got into a ferocious rhythm and she felt elated with the work.

I am high on digging, she thought.

Faster and faster she worked. High on digging and high on sex as well.

But she had never done this kind of work before. The sweat began to pour out of her body. Her breath became labored. Her hands began to cramp.

Finally, she had to stop and rest. Maybe, she thought, I should not dig anymore until I plot out the garden on a piece of paper. She knew she wanted a flower perimeter and vegetables in the main area.

She knocked the dirt off her stainless steel spade and walked back into the barn.

Standing just inside the large sliding door, she looked around at her cavernous, never-ending project; at the scaffolding, at the haphazard shelving containing her possessions—books, tools, dishes, clothes.

She was suddenly flooded with a massive weakness; the strength seemed to whoosh out of her body.

She clutched the spade tightly.

The weakness passed.

Then came another wave of disability. Her neck became rigid. Her stomach began to churn.

"What have I done?" she screamed at her dogs, who had followed her back into the barn.

They cowered.

She repeated those words over and over again to herself.

Then she burst into crazy laughter.

"Dear, dear Nightingale!" she shouted. "I am sorry! I am sorry!" she screamed at the stove.

She tried to steady herself. She tried to push the hysteria away. She tried to reason with herself.

I am a sophisticated woman. I have had many affairs. I have slept with other women's husbands. It never bothered me before. And Allie wasn't even engaged to Nightingale anymore.

Why this eruption of self-loathing? Why this paralyzing lunatic guilt over one tiny indiscretion?

She stood erect, breathing heavily. The tenseness in her neck and the nausea began to ease.

But her eyes were filling with tears.

Again she scanned her surroundings. She was astonished at what she saw, at where she was.

The truth dribbled into her consciousness.

It was all a sham. It was all a failure.

Her long march from Manhattan to Hillsbrook, to a new life close to the soil, close to the animals, close to the vision of Thoreau and St. Francis and all those who sought escape from the city into some kind of wilderness . . . all of it was a sham. Failure. Dilettantism. Absurdity. Bad faith.

I am a fool with a fantasy and a stainless steel spade, she thought, smiling for the first time in ages. It was an eerie smile.

She suddenly felt very calm. She looked around again at her failure, at her fantasy, at the furniture of her rural delusions, at the scaffolding of her huge unfinished barn.

It was, however, merely that calm that always appears before the storm . . . before the breakdown.

And it did not last long.

A cry seemed to bubble out of her throat, and, grabbing the spade handle with both hands, she began to smash the shelves.

A clerk whom she didn't know was behind the front desk in the motel. He was a young, somewhat goofy-looking man wearing a red vest festooned with all kinds of ballpoint pens. He had bright red hair to match his vest.

Didi explained her situation: she wanted her belongings.

It took a while for the lightbulb to go off in his brain. When it did, he clapped his hands.

"Of course! You're the lady with the corpse."

Then he gallantly ushered her into the motel

office, which contained a highly shellacked fake wood floor, a huge gray steel desk, green files along one wall, and a pseudo black leather sectional sofa configured in a half-moon shape.

He tiptoed out of the room and left her alone.

Her belongings were waiting for her, stacked neatly on the sofa.

Except for the sweater, of course. That was no doubt in a police lab somewhere.

It was such a lovely brown sweater—soft, warm wool.

How grotesque that it had been used to strangle a man!

The lamb that was sheared for it would be very sad, she thought.

At that thought, Dr. Nightingale became very uneasy.

A bevy of images coalesced.

A wool sweater.

A tethered lamb.

A bar called Green Pastures.

She contemplated the images for a moment. Strange. Too strange to have any significance. They had to be just randomly converging coincidences—like similar symptoms of divergent bovine disorders.

She picked up her luggage and headed for home.

She stopped. The attaché case was too light. She brought it back to the sofa and opened it. The manuscript was gone.

She threw the valise on the sofa and opened that. No manuscript.

She searched the office. No manuscript.

She rushed out and ran up and down the halls until she found the chambermaid.

The woman told her a bag of tattered paper had been thrown into the Dumpster in the alley.

Didi yelled at her: "Why did you do that!"

"I found it in the bathtub and it looked like junk to me," the chambermaid replied aggressively.

Didi ran to the alley and flung open the heavy-lidded Dumpster. She waded through the garbage until she found the relevant black plastic bag.

She brought it back to the office and dumped the contents on the floor.

What a mess it was! No wonder the chambermaid had thrown it away.

Someone had trashed the manuscript with a vengeance. Pages were ripped, stained, torn, and crumpled. A red marker had inscribed obscenities on dozens of pages.

She couldn't bring it home this way. She took a roll of cellophane tape from the attaché case, sat down on the floor amid the rubble, and began to reconstruct it as best she could.

As she reconstructed it physically, she mentally reconstructed the history of said manuscript since she had checked into the motel.

Obviously there had been two different assaults on it by two or more persons.

She didn't know who the first reader was, but he or she had merely stained it a bit with coffee while perusing it. And he or she had either found some way to break into the room or used a passkey.

The second reader—or rather, readers—had bribed their way into the room. She knew who they were: Ann Huggins and Arthur Bremen. They had reacted to it with a fury.

Of course, she contradicted herself, the two separate incidents *could* have been the work of *one* reader.

But the modes of entry and reading styles were widely divergent.

It was perplexing. None of the scenarios made sense because she didn't know the impetus for the reading.

She concentrated on the physical reconstruction now. Smoothing, rearranging in sequence, and taping ripped pages.

Only one small section of the manuscript was not ripped or crumpled.

This was a case history of a race horse brought to the Mid-Florida Equine Clinic with severe foreleg lameness stemming from radial nerve paralysis.

This disorder used to be common among carriage and draft horses working on wet cobblestones.

Now it appeared primarily on horses running a lot over muddy racecourses.

Traditionally, the only treatment was prolonged rest, with a 50-50 prognosis for cure.

The case history in Eleazar Wynn's manuscript, however, claimed he treated the horse quickly and successfully with some very advanced laser techniques.

Didi noted that while this section was not torn or crumpled, it had received the full force of the reader's venom.

Obscenities were scrawled across many of the pages along with crude diagrams, particularly small circles, crosses, and swastikas.

It was the group of circles—usually three together, sometimes touching—that riveted her attention.

She began to feel a profound uneasiness.

She remembered the circles Detective Nova

had described to her—the ones stamped on the murderous letter openers.

Could they be one and the same? A constantly reappearing logo of death?

She laughed nervously, closed her eyes, and then stared at the circles again.

She was missing something important, she knew. This was a section of the manuscript about a crippled racehorse.

Concentrate! she urged herself. Look! Look at the whole animal, not the symptoms alone.

She laughed again. This time not nervously but robustly, laughing at her own stupidity.

Racehorses have trainers. Trainers work for owners. Owners incorporate themselves as racing stables. Racing stables have identifying marks—designs and names that are registered with the Jockey Club, and which appear on their jockeys, horses, and barns.

These circles might be the design on a jockey's shirt, the "racing silks" that he wore when he rode for that stable.

She rushed to the phone and dialed New York City Information. She got the number for the Jockey Club, dialed it, and was put through to the records librarian.

Dr. Nightingale claimed that she was a veterinarian trying to locate horses she had treated in the past pursuant to a long-range study of longevity in racehorses.

The records librarian in New York, a soft-spoken gentleman, bought the fake story enthusiastically. Didi then laid out her information needs: the particulars about a racing stable that used "silks" containing two or perhaps three circles on a solid background.

"Are the circles themselves solid or lined?" the man asked.

"Lined," Didi responded, meaning that only a perimeter line was drawn—the inside was blank, allowing the background color to show through.

He asked her to hold on. He came back in three minutes and announced that he could find no such information. "Do you want me to try the dead file? It's easy to do now because it's all on computer," he said.

"Yes, by all means."

This time he came back very quickly. Yes, he found two outfits that had those silks in the past, but neither of them was currently racing.

Lionheart Stables. A California outfit that raced at Santa Anita. Three black circles on a white background.

Juniper House Stables. Ran in Florida at Gulfstream Park and Tampa Bay Downs. Four white circles on a red background.

Didi processed the information fast and made her decision quickly. It had to be the Florida one, because the tracks in Florida are muddier than their California counterparts and the horse in the case history suffered from a condition stemming from muddy tracks.

She asked for more information on the Florida operation.

Again the librarian left the phone. Again he returned swiftly. Only this time he said he could give out no further information without a written request.

She thanked him, hung up, dialed Florida Information, and called the Racing Secretary of Gulfstream Park. She asked for information on Juniper House Stables, which used to race at Gulfstream.

He had the answer at his fingertips, apparently.

"A small operation," he said. "Same owner and trainer: Suzanne Marks. In their last year of operation, maybe three or four years ago, they ran three horses . . . at most."

"Can you give me the names of the horses?"

This time he had to look up the information. It took him a while, but when he came back to the phone, he handed her equine diamonds.

"Lambchop. Lambshank. Lambpie."

Didi hung up the phone.

She sat down on the sofa, pale and suddenly exhausted. Oh, she knew a few things now.

These murders had everything to do with race-horses.

And racehorses were about money, big money.

And Ann Huggins was not on her way down to Florida.

Oh no, not yet. She had someone else to kill, in Atlantic City.

Charlie Gravis sat grimly in his small room off the hall, digesting what he had eaten of Mrs. Tunncy's noodles, cottage cheese, and butter supper.

He had tried to eat as little as possible, but he had to eat enough to avoid her suspicion.

He studied the clock face on his card table. It appeared to read fifteen minutes after six.

He was weary but excited. What a day it had been! What a night it was going to be!

He had successfully enlisted the pig man as maitre d'. Invitations to twenty upper-crust Hillsbrook couples had been delivered, asking them to arrive at Ike's Place, the new restaurant in town, at 8 P.M., to sample free the unveiling of a long-lost rural cuisine.

At seven o'clock Luis, Burt, Ike, and himself were to assemble for the final run-through. When the diners arrived—Charlie figured five or six couples would respond—everything must be ready.

At the last moment, however, Charlie had decided to add a wrinkle—a young waiter. That meant Trent Tucker had to be recruited. So now Charlie was waiting for him to return to his room.

He heard the door slam at six twenty-five. Charlie walked out of his own room, knocked on the young man's door, and went inside.

Trent Tucker was lying on his bed leafing through a gun magazine.

"Want to earn twenty bucks for three hours' work?" Charlie asked.

"When?"

"Now."

Tucker grinned sardonically: "You tell me, old man. Why should I work for you for a lousy twenty, when the boss gave me a hundred just because she likes me?"

"She gave everyone a hundred. And yours is probably gone already."

"That's for me to know and you to find out."

"Then why don't you just do it for me as a favor? All you have to do is wait on a few tables."

"Whose restaurant?"

"Mine. And Ike's."

Trent Tucker guffawed.

"Have you entered the dream world, Charlie?"

"Shut up and listen. I don't have time to argue with you or beg you. Our restaurant opens tonight. We remodeled Ike's barn. It'll be easy work. No orders to take. No appetizers. No desserts. No drinks. Just a few tables and all you do is bring three large main dishes to each table. It's family style, get it? Maybe you'll have to pour some water also. But that's about it."

Trent Tucker seemed to be considering the offer. That was enough for Charlie. He opened Trent's closet and pulled a blue shirt off a hanger. "Put it on now! And let's go."

Not only did Trent Tucker go but he drove Charlie over without a single wisecrack.

By seven o'clock the staff was resplendently assembled.

Luis Ragobert had on a starched white butcher's smock. He looked like the conductor of a celestial slaughterhouse. In his hands he held the menus, written in longhand, in rust crayon, by the poet's arthritic fingers.

Ike was wearing a 1960s-style porkpie hat and his Empire State Building souvenir tie.

Burt Conyers had tied his long hair in a pony-tail.

As for Charlie himself, all he had done for the

big night was to put on his wedding shoes and the plaid jacket he had bought for the memorial service for Dr. Nightingale's mother.

"The dining room looks real authentic," Charlie noted.

Ike grunted. "Most of the utensils don't match. Neither do the plates."

"Diversity is a prize beyond rubies," said Conyers.

One of the remaining cows in the barn began to methodically stomp the side of her pen.

The staff repaired to the front door of the barn, where they stood under the just-hoisted sign—an old yellow tablecloth with IKE'S PLACE done up in blue housepaint. Badian had put up the sign in spite of Charlie's protestations that the hip places remain signless. The cloth flapped in the breeze.

"Like the wings of a dove," the poet noted.

They waited silently.

At seven-thirty Ike began to get nervous. "Where the hell are they?"

"Have patience," Charlie consoled. "Upper-crust people always arrive late."

At ten to eight Ike lit a cigar and gave one to the pig farmer, who just chewed it, his eyes narrowing.

At eight o'clock Ike moaned: "I expected at least one!"

Charlie was about to buttress his partner's faith again, when suddenly, from the road, came the unmistakable front lights of a vehicle moving onto the Badian property.

And then another. And another. And three more after them!

"My friends!" Charlie shouted. "We have hit paydirt!"

Didi looked at the clock dial, which sent out greenish rays in the dark. It was eight-thirty in the evening.

How many hours had she been lying on that bed in that motel? Many. Since three o'clock, at least, when she had checked into a new room.

The manager wasn't happy with her decision to stay. He was obviously very nervous about guests who entertained corpses even if said guests were only tangentially implicated.

So she had spent the afternoon and early evening on the bed of her new room, recovering from what had to be recovered from, reading and rereading the case history of the lame horse, closing her eyes and thinking of peculiar lambs, and taking ferocious little naps with the lights on and the lights off.

Many, many times she had been on the verge of calling Detective Nova. But she hadn't. It was somehow not appropriate. He would find her analysis lacking demonstrable facts. He was sure where the trail now led: Florida.

There was another reason she hadn't called. Did was certain that she had leapt—however inadvertently—into the true heart of the equine darkness that constituted the horrible murders. But no matter how many times she confirmed it to herself, her rational mind remained anxious. Too many bizarre things had fallen into place too quickly—all emerging from a crushed and mutilated manuscript. Yes, she was uneasy.

Once, during the day, she had ventured outside and brought back two jelly donuts and a coffee. That was all she had eaten all day, yet she wasn't hungry.

Now, as the time to act approached—the time to catch the killer as the killer cornered her next and last victim—Didi realized she needed a weapon.

The only thing available in her kit was a hoof pick—an ugly little chisel-like tool with a wooden handle, used by blacksmiths and vets to clean out a horse's hoof.

It would have to do. She changed into jeans, a sweatshirt, and boots. She fastened a bandanna around her head to give herself a little pizzazz and to change her appearance.

Other than stomach queasiness, only two things bothered her as she headed for the board-walk entrance of Wonderland Casino.

First, would she recognize Ann Huggins if she saw her? She tried to reconstruct the woman, but all she could remember was her height—Huggins was unusually tall—and her stoop, and her straggly blond hair, and a vague sense of too much makeup. She could not recall the face.

This is a pseudo problem, she finally realized. When she saw Ann Huggins again, she damn well would know her.

The second problem was thornier. Why was she so sure that the next victim of Ann Huggins would be the young Asian shoe clerk cum gambler?

It had not been revealed to her like the tablets on Mt. Sinai. To get to that point, she had simply thrown away the ephemera—like lamb imagery and letter openers—and tried to isolate the core.

The core was surely exposed. The murders were about racehorses. Racehorses were about money—purses, syndication, breeding. And the financial base of the racing industry was gambling.

There was another core factor. Hadn't Lucien Harmony spent his nights the same way as Wu? In the horse room of Wonderland Casino?

They were both winners. They both gambled in one place. At different times. Wu seemed to be Harmony's successor. One dead. One about to be.

She walked into the casino and up to the horse room. It was more crowded than the last time. Wu—Jack or John, she still didn't know for sure— was seated at the same table, displaying the same calm manner.

This time, Didi didn't sit. She kept close to one wall, standing erect, letting her eyes scan the room back and forth. Drinks were offered. She declined.

She placed the hoof pick in the sleeve of her sweatshirt so that it was readily accessible.

As she perused the scene, she had a growing feeling that her instincts were correct. This was where the dragon lady would strike again. Probably with her letter opener. Wu was the perfect victim in the perfect place. He was seated. His thoughts were somewhere else. The woman could walk by, drive the spike into his neck, and be gone before anyone knew what was happening.

Wu would be lamb chops.

Why was she making bad jokes?

She stood against the wall, vigilant, for only an hour.

Then things turned very peculiar.

Wu's manner changed abruptly. He seemed to be losing his cool, becoming agitated, going back and forth between betting machines, television screens, and his table.

He had also started to use a cell phone continuously. Didi hadn't seen him with one the first time she was in the horse room. And Wu had started drinking. One after another.

Does he know? Had he spotted her in the crowd? Either Nightingale or Huggins?

She was reminded of her mother's favorite song. That enchanted evening one—the lyrics escaped her at the moment but the tune was still with her.

Suddenly Wu got up and walked out.

Didi followed him. Wu was becoming more and more agitated. He walked downstairs and began feeding coins into slot machines. He went from one to another like a deranged man in an automat. He was moving so quickly that he seemed not even to wait for the results of one pull of the machine before moving on to the next.

Then he was calm again, totally. The agitation

had vanished. He stood quietly in front of a machine and just stared.

He walked out of the casino and onto the boardwalk.

Didi followed and snuggled against the building.

Wu breathed deeply and lifted his arms skyward—body language for "What a beautiful evening."

The boardwalk was now dense with people walking arm in arm. Many were going from one casino to another to try their luck. Several couples had the unmistakable look of honeymooners.

Wu walked to the railing and leaned his arms on it, staring out at the beach, the ocean, the stars.

He seemed to be in a state of transfixed quietude.

Then the horror!

From the midst of the strolling crowd emerged a tall figure, moving fast to the railing.

When the figure reached down and grasped Wu's legs, Didi knew it was *her*! She yelled out to Wu: "Look behind you!" as she sprinted toward the railing.

Wu was sent hurtling over the rail to the beach—screaming.

The assailant leaped over the rail after him.

Didi followed, the hoof pick now in her hand. It was a steeper drop than she'd imagined. The landing jarred her, but only for a moment. Wu was running along the beach, the assailant following him and gaining, her weapon high in the air.

"Ann Huggins! Ann Huggins!" Didi kept screaming the name, hoping the identification would forestall the carnage.

Wu fell.

Ann was on him, both hands around the weapon, which was raised high over her head.

Didi reached the pair as the letter opener started its descent.

She drove the hoof pick into the back of Huggins's thigh.

The assailant moaned and fell forward onto the sand.

Didi, too, fell, from the shock of driving the weapon into a human leg. A cracking sound exploded in her ear! Then another.

A man was standing three feet from her, firing a pistol into the air. The weapon was in his left hand. In his right hand he held an open identification wallet.

"No one move! No one move!" he yelled.

Didi stared at Ann Huggins writhing on the sand, the pick still in her thigh.

Ann tried uselessly to raise herself from the sand. It was only then that Didi could see something was wrong—very wrong.

The person twisting with pain was not Ann Huggins. It wasn't even a woman. It was a black man in a chauffeur's outfit.

The man with the gun knelt down beside Didi: "Are you okay, Dr. Nightingale?"

"Yes. Who are you?"

"I'm Loughlin. The state trooper assigned to you. I've been following you since you arrived in Atlantic City."

"By whose order?"

"Nova's."

It suddenly dawned on Didi that the first sloppy reader of Eleazar Wynn's manuscript was probably this state trooper—on Nova's instructions, as part of the investigation. That made sense. Her body was trembling slightly. It was a bit hard to breathe. She stared at the trooper. She didn't really mind that he had been following her. Not now. And she had sensed that someone was in the shadows all the time; she had felt it and articulated it to herself. But the room invasion surprised her.

"Don't you know it's illegal to enter my room without a warrant?" she asked in a flat voice. It felt good to deal with such a minor matter in the midst of all the major mayhem.

The trooper smiled, a bit mockingly. "This is Atlantic City, lady. Different rules."

No truer words were ever said, she thought.

Then she looked casually at the man she had stabbed. He was silent and still. Wu, however, was gasping for breath from his run.

"I know you," she said quietly to the black man. "Your name is Moe Brady."

She felt the state trooper's arm under hers, lifting her up. "The tide is coming in," he said.

Eleven couples had shown up for Charlie and Ike's feast. Since there were only ten tables, the eleventh had been quickly constructed out of an old door from Ike's junk heap.

The diners were now deep into their repasts. Things were not merely going well—they were going spectacularly.

There was a low hum from the diners as they first sampled each dish and then took generous helpings of the long-lost cuisine. Charlie interpreted their almost beatific countenances as much more than just joy in a good meal; they were participating in culinary history.

The staff had performed like pros. Trent Tucker was a superlative waiter. The pig man was the soul of concern and elegance. The poet, exiled to the kitchen in the house lest he do something foolish, had maintained the food at the proper temperature prior to its being served. Ike, who was in charge of nothing and everything, had socialized with the guests, distributing cryptic gems of conviviality.

Even the four remaining cows in the barn were playing their roles to perfection. They understood that they had to bellow once in a while to guarantee authenticity—after all, this was a dairy barn. And they did so, with the deep resonance of distress.

Charlie stayed in the shadows and monitored the customers: Mr. and Mrs. Plumb; Mr. and Mrs. Dannigalt; Mr. and Mrs. Browner; Mary Kreeger and her brother Larry; old Mrs. Jakes and her daughter Beth. There were others whom he could not name off the top of his head. They all knew one another, of course, but there was little conversation among tables. This was good, Charlie knew. It meant the cuisine had mesmerized them.

What a genius that man is, Charlie thought, thinking of the poet. It was Burt Conyers who had revealed the cuisine, and the power and subtlety of it was so great that even two hapless cooks like Ike and Charlie could not ruin the end product.

Charlie walked out of the barn to savor his triumph in solitude. Trent Tucker, however, was also outside, smoking a cigarette.

"I got to hand it to you, Charlie. I mean, you and Ike got yourself a winner," Trent said.

"It's only the beginning," Charlie noted nonchalantly. "We'll open next in Rhinebeck, then Manhattan, then L.A. Hell, we can even start franchising European operations."

"Maybe someone'll ask you to do a cookbook, Charlie."

"No doubt. Maybe we'll even market the cuisine in supermarkets. Can you see it, kid? Ike's Place Frozen Foods all over the country."

Suddenly Beth Jakes walked out of the barn. She whispered in Charlie's ear: "I need a ladies room."

Charlie felt as if he'd been kicked in the head by a cow. How could he have been so stupid? Why hadn't he thought about bathroom facilities? Diners couldn't step out the back door of the barn and piss into the wind, like Ike and he did all the time.

His agitation vanished as quickly as it had erupted. The house! Of course! She could use the bathroom in the house.

He pointed the way. "Just walk through the front door and head for the back of the house.

Just before you reach the kitchen, there's a bathroom on the right."

Beth headed for the house. Trent Tucker finished his cigarette and went back inside the barn. Charlie followed him.

Not more than sixty seconds passed before they heard bloodcurdling screams coming from the direction of the house.

Everyone started running, jamming the exit of the barn. Charlie and Ragobert got out first.

As Charlie chugged the best he could to the house, all he could think of was the poet. Burt was manning the kitchen. He must have attacked the girl. He must have savaged the girl in some way. He must have exposed himself. Oh, that broken-down drunken idiot!

The screams were weaker now, but they kept on coming.

Trent Tucker passed Charlie and started to kick at the door.

It swung open and the poet was standing there, wearing an apron, looking confused.

Charlie yelled, "What the hell is happening, Burt?"

"I haven't the slightest idea. But there is a lot of noise," he replied.

They all ran to the bathroom. The hysterical young woman was standing there, trembling.

Her voice was too hoarse to scream anymore with authority—a series of bleats emerged.

She pointed to the bathtub.

In it were the corpses of five woodchucks.

Two were headless.

One was eviscerated.

One was skinned.

One was a complete corpse and almost blissful in demeanor.

Other diners piled into the bathroom. One by one they glanced into the tub.

Charlie, in his wisdom, tried to diffuse the situation. He addressed them in a kindly fashion, with a hint of pride: "As you can see, folks, we use only fresh ingredients."

It was, alas, the wrong thing to say. The diners fled the house, and Ike's Place. The cuisine had lost all its charms—irrevocably.

Chapter 9

Troopers Nova and Loughlin arrived at Didi's motel at 7 A.M.

They were unkempt and obviously exhausted. They brought cold coffee.

The troopers stood as Didi, seated on the edge of the bed, spoke into the tape recorder on the end table.

She had given them a preliminary statement after last night's beach incident. Now she elaborated, detailing why she had been there: how she had arrived at the belief that Wu would be the next victim; all the facts she had obtained from the calls to the Jockey Club and Gulfstream Park; and her tying together the lambs, the weapons, and the horses from a reading of the Wynn manuscript.

When she had finished, Nova said, "You came

very close to the whole ball of wax. I'm much impressed."

"Thank you. But look. What I just spoke into your machine made me sound like a pontificating idiot. Like I was a brilliant criminal investigator. Now that the machine is turned off, let me get a little closer to the truth. I really can't claim that it was other than an informed hunch. A hunch based on my knowledge of the racetrack and its people. I may be young, but believe me, I've worked around racetracks. I know them. There were all kinds of vague signifiers floating around me.

"It was obvious to me that the person who had marked the manuscript with such a fury had killed. And he'd killed because of something that had happened in a racing stable, concerning a racehorse—Lambchop. That's what the lamb imagery in and around all the corpses had to be about. Now, it's not uncommon for trainers and vets to get into violent arguments. But Lambchop had been cured and made sound by Wynn and his staff. Nothing made sense. Then I remembered Harmony. What was his connection? He was a gambler. Why did he die? The poor man just gambled. Mind you, I am trying to reconstruct now how I came to the hunch. I mean, I don't specifically remember thinking it out at the time.

"But the moment I thought of Harmony, I felt he could fit in only one way. He was betting on horses not for himself—for someone else. And then the hunch became concrete. Gambling money rules the Thoroughbred horse world. Every bloody aspect of it. But gamblers are as replaceable as tissues. If the mess was about gambling, Harmony had to have a successor. And the logical successor was Wu. Same casino. Same hours. And Wu had been present when Wynn was murdered. That is how I think I constructed the ball of wax."

"But I don't think you have a clue as to how the wax got melted."

"Please enlighten me."

Both troopers laughed.

"Sure, I will," Nova said, "but what I'm going to tell you is what we wrung out of Brady and Wu. When we get hold of the others, the story might change."

"I want to know now. I deserve to know."

"Yes, you do, Dr. Nightingale. So here's what we got."

He sat down on a window ledge before he spoke again.

"Maybe you ought to get it right from the

horse's mouth. Maybe you ought to hear the verbatim record. Why not? What do you think, Loughlin?"

"It's irregular."

Nova found that funny. "Let her hear it!" he ordered. "Brady first."

Loughlin removed the cassette that had recorded Didi. He clicked in another one and pressed the "play" button.

Didi hunched over, anxious to hear everything clearly.

Nova: Do you understand what the charges are
  against you?

Brady: I couldn't care less.

Nova: For starters—assault with a deadly weapon
  and assault with intent to kill.

Brady: So?

Nova: We did a check. Your name isn't Moe Brady.
  Your fingerprints are registered with the
  Florida Racing Authority. You were an assistant trainer at Gulfstream Park. And your real
  name is Samuel Hockenberry.

Brady: You get the brass ring.

Nova: Why did you attack John Wu?

Brady: Simple. I wanted to kill him. Like I killed
  the others.

Nova: Others? Whoa! Are you admitting to multiple murders?

Brady: Happily.

Nova: Can you give me the names of these victims?

Brady: Sure. Lucien Harmony. Eleazar Wynn. Milo Kraft. Arthur Bremen.

Nova: Why did you kill them?

Brady: For the same reason as Wu.

Nova: Which is . . . ?

Brady: They earned it.

Nova: What the hell does that mean?

Brady: It's a long story and I'm tired.

Nova: But I'm wide awake. Besides, the more you help me now, the more I can help you later.

Brady: You think I'm an idiot? I'm a dead man. Who cares if it goes easier? At worst I'll get three consecutive life terms. At best I'll get a lethal injection. Then I'll die happy. Maybe whistling "gonna take a sentimental journey." You hear me. You understand. Whatever you do to me is fine. Believe me, it was worth it.

Nova: Talk to me, Brady. You're not a psycho. Tell me why. Where does this kind of hate come from?

Brady: From Juniper House Stables. From Suzanne and Jamie and Lambchop.

Nova: Come on, man, talk sense!

Brady: Juniper House was a racing stable at Gulfstream. Owned and operated by Suzanne
Marx. It was a dream of an outfit.

Nova: You mean it made big money?

Brady: No! No! It just broke even. But it was a
dream outfit. Suzanne Marx bred and trained
the horses. Never more than three or four in
the barn. Claiming horses, for the most part.
Once in a while an Allowance horse. Her
daughter, Jamie, rode for her. Her other
daughter, Maria, groomed. I was assistant
trainer and a whole lot more.

Nova: What does that mean—"a whole lot more"?

Brady: Her husband was dead. Suzanne and I
were lovers. And I guess I was kind of a sur-
rogate father to her girls. Yeah, it was the best
of times. And then the shit began to happen.

Nova: What does all this have to do with four
murders and one attempted murder?

Brady: Nothing. But then Lambchop, one of her
horses, went lame.

Nova: So?

Brady: So Suzanne shipped him to the Mid-
Florida Equine Clinic. She had heard good
things about the place. The horse came back
real fit, ready to run. Suzanne put him in a
claiming race, just to condition him. We didn't
expect anything after a two-month layoff.

Lambchop went off at sixty-to-one odds. He blew the other horses out of the water—winning by five lengths. We had a helluva celebration. Suzanne ran him in two more cheap races. He lost bad. Then she gave him a month's rest and ran him again. He went off at thirty-to-one odds. He was way ahead, twenty yards from the wire. Then he went down and the jockey went with him.

Nova: What happened to them?

Brady: The horse broke a leg. He was destroyed on the track. Jamie was taken off on a gurney with a broken back, paralyzed. A week later we found out there was no chance of recovery. She would be a vegetable more or less until the day she died.

Nova: A sad story. But that's horse racing.

Brady: So they say. Anyway, it gets sadder. Suzanne went around the bend. She couldn't handle what happened to her daughter. She hooked up a vacuum cleaner hose to the exhaust pipe of her Honda Civic, closed the windows, turned on the ignition, and killed herself. That was the end of Juniper House Stables.

Nova: What happened to the other horses?

Brady: We sold them. We sold everything. But the money went quick, taking care of Jamie.

When we ran out, we declared bankruptcy and filed for Medicaid for her. We got her into a rehab facility. Six months later, she finally was able to speak a real sentence. And that was the beginning of the end for those bastards.

Nova: Which bastards?

Brady: Mid-Florida Equine. Jamie told us some very strange things that had happened during Lambchop's last race. The horse had suddenly started accelerating and then slowing down, speeding up and then braking. All the while he was changing leads. Now, Jamie and Marie are young. This didn't mean anything to them. But I had been around the racetracks a long time and the minute I heard her describe the way the horse was running, I thought . . . *buzzer!*

Nova: Buzzer? What do you mean, buzzer?

Brady: It's a small, primitive shocking device, operated by battery. Nobody dares use them anymore, but it was the gimmick of choice for crooked trainers and jockeys a while back. A jockey would hide it on his person and shock the horse during a critical part of the race—usually around the far turn—to get the horse to accelerate. The tracks cracked down. If they found a buzzer on a jockey, he was banned from racing for life. And many were.

Nova: Are you saying Jamie Marx did that to her mother's horse?

Brady: Of course not. It just set me to thinking. Something bad had happened to that horse. During the race. Something crooked . . . twisted . . . inexplicable . . . had occurred which killed the horse and maimed the rider. And I had this strange gut feeling that it had something to do with the Mid-Florida veterinary clinic. That's where Lambchop had been treated and cured of his lameness. But had he been "cured"? Of course. Maybe more than cured.

In his first race after coming back, he won at odds of sixty-to-one. I didn't have any proof. I didn't have any concrete facts. And I didn't have the slightest idea what they had done to him. It was just a suspicion that got stronger and stronger. Finally, Maria agreed with me.

We hatched a very simple plan. We had nothing at all to lose, not anymore. Maria was to become Mary Alonso and get a job at the Mid-Florida Equine Clinic. She got the job fast. The first thing she found out was that the owners were big spenders. Yachts. Planes. Cars. Banquets. Trips to Europe. And land. They had bought up a dozen farms in the county—most of them with Black Angus beef cattle heads.

Yes, they were making big money and spending even bigger money all over the place. The longer Maria stayed there, the more she felt I was right. But she found nothing that could implicate them in the destruction of Juniper House Stables. She just wasn't privy to their secrets. So she took the next logical step. She made herself sexually available to both Bremen and Wynn. They couldn't get enough of her. She began to party with them and travel with them. And finally it paid off. A slip of the tongue here. A misplaced comment there. Cryptic messages. Odd veterinary records. The whole stinking mess began to take shape.

Nova: You mean she was able to confirm the thing—the thing with the buzzer?

Brady: Not really. The people who ran the equine clinic gave the lowly buzzer a very high-tech, coast-to-coast twist. Certain horses that came to their clinics were fitted with tiny metal strips in their braided manes before they were returned to their stables. The owner and trainers, of course, knew nothing about the implants. When the horses ran again, they would go off at enormous odds because of their lay-offs. When they ran, one of the clinic's operatives—like Ann Huggins—would be in the stands. It was a variation on *The Manchurian*

Candidate. The operative used a tiny portable transmitter to send a signal to the metal strip embedded in the mane, which translated into a profound shock to the horse, which always resulted in an astonishing burst of speed. The burst would not last long. The horse would slow. Again the signal was sent. Again the shock. And so it went.

Nova: How many horses were involved?

Brady: Must have been dozens. Horses were shipped to the clinic for treatment from virtually every track in the U.S. and Canada.

Nova: How were the bets placed?

Brady: Only in Atlantic City. That's where I went first. To kill the man who placed the bets for them—Lucien Harmony.

Nova: And Jack Wu was his successor?

Brady: Exactly.

Nova: Was Wynn's wife involved in the scam?

Brady: Yes.

Nova: And Milo Kraft?

Brady: No.

Nova: Then why did you kill him?

Brady: He was hired as a private detective to find Lucien's murderer. The Wynns hired him. They were frightened. Kraft was good. He was getting too close for comfort.

Nova: So you and this Mary Alonso, or whatever

the hell her name is, are traveling around the country like butchering Bonnies and Clydes. You and she were rolling up the scam operation, body by body.

Brady: I killed them all—alone. Maria was not involved.

Nova: Do you really expect me to believe that? Where is she now?

Brady: Ten thousand miles away, I hope.

Nova: What about that eighteen-month gap between the murder of Harmony and the murder of Eleazar Wynn?

Brady: After I killed Harmony, Jamie began to show improvement, as if by magic. She could move her limbs a bit, feel certain sensations in her body. We thought perhaps there would be at least a partial recovery. The signs were there. So I watched and waited. I was all she had. Maria was still working at Mid-Florida Equine. I borrowed money from a loanshark and got Jamie into a good rehab center. Then she crashed again. This time deeper into her paralysis. It was like watching a suffering rag doll.

Nova: Why didn't you just blow them away with a shotgun? Why the exotic stuff with the murder weapon? Why all that symbolic garbage?

Brady: Garbage? Oh no, my friend. They murdered Suzanne, didn't they? Suzanne loved letter openers. She collected them. She had dozens of them made up with the stable's racing silk design on them. She gave them out as gifts. So I gave it to them—as gifts—in the neck.

And they murdered Lambchop with Jamie on his back, didn't they? So I gave them Lambchop back. A bar called Green Pastures where Harmony and other lambs of God frolicked in a whiskey haze. A toy lamb staked out near Kraft's body. A lambswool sweater wrapped around Bremen's neck. Poor man, he probably wanted a letter opener, but I didn't have one handy. So I had to brain him with a telephone. All this, garbage? No! Not by a long shot. Poetic justice, as they say. And those who were about to die, those who were running from me, became more and more frightened. They knew they were going to die and they knew why.

Detective Nova made a cutting motion with his hand. Loughlin stopped the tape.

"Play the second part of the Wu tape," Nova ordered.

Loughlin did as he was told, quickly replacing cassettes.

Nova: Why should we believe anything you tell us, Mr. Wu? You lied to us about the Wynn murder.

Wu: No, I didn't.

Nova: Sure you did. You told us you didn't know anyone in the shoe store at the time of the murder except the other store clerk. But, in fact, you were working for both Eleazar Wynn and Ann Huggins, weren't you? You were placing bets for them.

Wu: Yes, I was working for them. But I had never laid eyes on either of them before. I was phoned the day before and told that there would be a meeting in the store. They wanted to talk to me, in person. Since I had been using some of their money to make my own bets and was in to them for some money, I figured they were going to threaten me or work me over a bit. All they told me on the phone was that I would be met and talked to. When Huggins and the woman who saved my life on the beach came in together, I didn't know if either of them had anything to do with the operation.

In fact, it wasn't until much later that the Nightingale woman came up to me in the casino and I realized her questions were so stupid she couldn't have been part of the deal.

Remember—everything was done by phone. I never saw a face. Eleazar Wynn was just a customer to me, like the women were. Obviously they were about to identify themselves. But the killer aborted the meeting, didn't he?

Nova: Surely you weren't recruited on the phone.

Wu: OK. You're right. The interview was the only time I saw a face! But it wasn't one of the faces in the shoe store that day.

Nova: A man or a woman?

Wu: A woman.

Nova: Take a look at these photos. Is she there?

Wu: Yes! Her!

Nova: For the record, let it be noted that Mr. Wu identified Joy Wynn as the woman who recruited him. Now, tell me how the money was handled.

Wu: They set up a credit line for me at the casino. I would call prearranged numbers to get the races and tracks to bet. Half the winnings I took in cash. I wrapped the bills in horse leg bandages that were mailed to my house once a month; then I FedEx-ed the packages to a post office box in Florida. I was told to convert the money into fifty-dollar bills and never to mail more than two hundred bills in one package.

Nova: You're a sharp young man. So what I really

don't get is this: Surely you must have figured out that you were in great danger ... that some lunatics were hunting down all the people in your operation. Hell, your predecessor Harmony was murdered. The man investigating the murder was murdered. One of the architects of the scam, Eleazar Wynn, was murdered right in front of you. Didn't you see it coming toward you? Weren't you afraid? In fact, that meeting in the shoe store might not have been about you skimming profits. Maybe they were simply going to help you stay alive. After all, they needed you. You were the point man. You made the bets. You collected the money.

Wu: Listen! In the shoe store I make six dollars an hour. In the casino, on an average night, I make six hundred an hour. You see where I'm coming from, Detective?

The machine was shut off.

Didi stared at her boots. They were scruffy from the beach. The tapes had given her too much information to process.

But one thing was sorely lacking. She asked: "What about me?"

"I don't understand your question."

"Me! Me! Why were those people after me?"

"Look, Huggins probably just took you along to that shoe store for company, or as cover. But the killer who slipped in and out of that store in seconds probably saw you even though you didn't see him. He must have thought you were with the Clinic cabal. As for the Clinic people, they also became suspicious of you. My guess is that Milo didn't like your answers when he visited you in Hillsbrook. He called Joy Wynn. Then he followed you on the train. Brady was following him. When Milo was murdered in North Philadelphia, their suspicions increased. I think that's why Huggins and Bremen went to your motel room—they were looking for confirmation, maybe for letter openers. Maybe that's why the vet's wife gave you his manuscript in the first place . . . suspicion of you . . . who knows? I mean, even I thought you were involved somehow. That's why you were kept under surveillance. That's why we looked at the manuscript."

"And spilled coffee all over it."

"Sorry about that. It was dull reading. Told us nothing. Huggins and Bremen found nothing in your room either. Except an assassin. Huggins got away. Bremen didn't. I misinterpreted the facts. Huggins was running south, but not to kill. She was running away from *being* killed."

"What do I do with the money?" Didi asked.

"What money?"

"The money Joy Wynn has given me to do the manuscript."

"Keep it. That lady is going to do some time. Why don't you finish the manuscript, mail it to the clinic in Florida return receipt requested, and keep the damn money. You earned it." He laughed and added: "Or maybe call a lawyer."

"You know, the funny thing is that everything was in the manuscript. I mean, Lambchop was there, lame, and then being cured."

"Farfetched, Dr. Nightingale. Was there anything in the case history about a tiny piece of metal in a braided mane?"

"No. Well, yes and no. It lay there, hidden. It needed a flame. Brady gave me that flame when he marked the manuscript after killing Bremen in my room. It was the flame, the illumination of rage surrounding Lambchop, that gave me the hunch."

Loughlin chimed in for the first time: "Do you need that chisel back?"

"It's a hoof pick, not a chisel. But no, thanks. They're just nine ninety-five apiece at Agway."

The two troopers grinned at her. She didn't like the grin. They were telling her in their fashion that sweet Dr. Nightingale could be just as violent as any of them.

Oh yes. It was time to go home.

She felt no sense of triumph as she left, only sadness. So many seemingly intelligent and successful people had destroyed themselves. Eleazar Wynn was the saddest story. The man had been a total contradiction. On the one hand, he was a famous vet, doing groundbreaking work in the field of equine lameness. Yet at the same time, he was orchestrating a cruel and demonic race-fixing scheme. The motive was greed. But Didi had seen this contradiction before. It often surfaced in the world of Thoroughbred racing, although she didn't know why, really. She recalled the exercise rider she had met in Saratoga who would weep if a horse got hurt, but would "saw" the bit in a horse's mouth until blood flowed if the horse did not obey commands.

I must do a paper on this phenomenon one day, she thought.

Chapter 10

It was dark when she arrived at the house, but her elves were gathered outside to welcome her. Trent Tucker took her bags and led her into the kitchen, where Mrs. Tunney had prepared a supper buffet of cold cuts and store-bought chocolate cookies, along with coffee and tea.

Didi, suddenly hungry, made herself a huge sandwich and wolfed it down. Mrs. Tunney beamed with pleasure at this evidence of her healthy appetite.

Everyone, in fact, seemed happy except Charlie Gravis. That worried Didi. Had something bad happened in the practice? Had one of the covering vets screwed up? The moment she finished her sandwich, she began to interrogate him. No, it seemed nothing was wrong there. Not even a single emergency call while she was away. Not even a calf with a ripped ear.

She needed a nap in her own bed. She needed a shower. But before any of that, she needed to see Rose. She wanted to tell her friend just what had happened in Atlantic City.

"Give me the keys to the Jeep," she said to Charlie. He handed them to her.

She left immediately, ignoring the elfin protests, and drove to Rose Vigdor's place.

The property was quiet and dark. Rose must have let the stove go out—silly girl. And the dogs didn't seem to be around, so maybe she was in town.

I'll wait, Didi thought. She took her flashlight from the Jeep and pushed open the sliding door of the barn.

She could not believe what she saw. Her flashlight began to swing wildly in huge arcs.

Most of the books were gone. And the tea kettles. The mats were rolled up and piled one on top of another, as if they were being junked. The shelves that had held Rose's clothing were bare. Several shelves were splintered.

Didi moved deeper into the space. She heard a noise behind the cold stove.

"Rose! Rose! Is that you?" she shouted.

A man stepped out.

She became rigid with fear, holding the flashlight up like a weapon. Then she saw it was Allie Voegler.

"What the hell are you doing here, Allie? Where's Rose?"

"I don't know," he said.

Didi began to walk back and forth, trying to understand. "It looks like she left! Like she just up and left. What is going on?"

Voegler was silent.

"I'm asking you again. What are you doing here?"

"Paying a visit," he replied.

"Don't lie to me! You and Rose weren't even on speaking terms. Has something happened to her? Is she in trouble?"

Officer Albert Voegler didn't answer. Her flashlight caught something on the ground. She approached.

It was a disassembled .22 caliber rifle. And next to the carefully arranged stack of parts was an unopened bag of chips.

The way the objects lay there gave her the shivers. Crazy as it seemed, they had a kind of ritualistic, almost satanic quality.

"Do you know what this stuff is?" she asked him.

He didn't answer. He started out of the barn.

"Where are you going!" she screamed at him. "Talk to me! Tell me where she is!"

He kept on walking. He was gone.

I have to calm down, she thought. I am panicking. There are a hundred explanations. Maybe there's a call from her on my machine. Maybe a note from her is back at the house. Maybe she took a long drive on a whim. Rose will do things like that. Maybe she moved her belongings into storage because she wanted to finally paint or bring in electricity. Maybe, maybe, maybe.

Everything will be all right in the morning, Didi thought. Everything will become clear. Why wouldn't it? There is no crime here.

Dr. Nightingale flicked off her light and walked to the red Jeep.

She took the long route home, through the town of Hillsbrook. The quiet, empty streets seemed to calm her.

Then she caught sight of Allie's car parked in front of the Hillsbrook Pub.

She slowed down. She shouldn't have yelled at him. Allie had his own problems, what with the suspension and probation, not to mention the broken engagement. He'd probably been at Rose's place because he had spotted the red Jeep and followed it.

She parked and went in to apologize. Allie was

seated at the front end of the bar, alone, watching a basketball game on television.

She could feel his tension as she sat on the stool next to his. The bar was empty. The bartender came toward her; she waved him away. She noticed Allie was drinking whiskey along with his beer. Not good.

"Look, I'm sorry I screamed at you back there," she said. "I was worried about her, that's all. It's silly to worry, though. Rose can take care of herself. She always does things on the spur of the moment."

He still did not look at her.

"How did you like your vacation?" he asked.

"It wasn't a vacation and I didn't like it," she replied.

"Do you hate me, Didi?"

"Of course not."

"Do you want me out of Hillsbrook?"

"No."

"Do you want me out of your life?"

She didn't answer. She didn't know how to respond. She didn't know what she wanted.

He turned suddenly and put his hand lightly on her shoulder.

"I've been bad," he said. She thought he meant the whiskey. She searched his face. She'd been away only a few days, but he seemed to have aged ten years.

His face came closer. His hand tightened on her shoulder.

"Let me hold you," he whispered. And then he pulled her toward him.

She wrenched free so suddenly and with such force that he jerked back in horror and sent the whiskey glass spinning off the bar.

The bartender glared at them but did nothing.

Allie recovered. She recovered. He walked to the jukebox and played Patsy Cline singing "Crazy." He didn't return to the bar. Instead, he stood there, his back to her, listening.

Why am I so cruel to this man? she thought. Why can't I love him as he loves me? Why won't I let him hold me? What kind of idiot have I become?

A sudden thought seemed to wash over her: how fragile everything is. It can all vanish in a moment, like that moment Lambchop's leg snapped.

She slipped off the barstool and walked over to Allie. She pulled playfully at the back of his shaggy head. He turned, lifted her a few inches off the floor, and they began to dance.

As she trudged through the thick, sweet-smelling ground cover toward the herd of grazing bovines, Didi for some reason thought of an old piece of nonsense verse:

> There once was a cow named Priscilla
> Her milk came out sarsaparilla
> She waited for dark
> And then started to bark
> And that's why we hired a gorilla

What a stupid ditty, she thought, but to be among cows always made her childish. Particularly in a field in late summer. Sweet black-and-white beasts dotting the green, green grass. It was like living in a beautiful watercolor painting. Didi winced at her misplaced romanticism. She was, after all, Dr. Deirdre Quinn Nightingale,

DVM, a working vet going to visit a sick cow—
not a whimsical travel writer.

Walking beside her was a gawky middle-aged
woman named Lee Ayers. This was her cow farm,
and it was called precisely that—The Cow Farm.
It was Didi's first visit to the farm, and first meeting with Lee, but she had heard of Mrs. Ayers
and her operation. Lee Ayers was one of several
people who had started up small "organic" dairy
farms amidst the ruins of the commercial dairy
industry in Dutchess County.

They were nothing like their failed predeces-
sors. They had very small herds. They fed the
cows no commercial feed. They avoided all anti-
biotics. They milked in a primitive fashion, with
old-fashioned pails. They delivered the milk
themselves to a small cooperative processing
plant. They put the milk in bottles, not cartons.
They didn't sell the milk in supermarkets, only
in posh suburban and big-city gourmet shops.
They rode the nostalgia wave like surfers.

Dr. Nightingale had made no judgment on
them one way or the other. Cows were cows, and
the more the merrier. In one area, in fact, the new
dairy people had gained her respect. They knew
how to plant and rotate fodder and grazing
crops—clover, alfalfa, rye. Their cows ate well.

Charlie Gravis, Didi's geriatric veterinary assistant, was walking behind the two women, wheezing and cursing under his breath, the "rounds bag" under his right arm.

Didi smiled at his behavior. The morning was already warm, but it wasn't the summer heat that was making him irascible. The old dairy farmer hated anything to do with the word "organic." It drove him into an unreasoning fury.

Suddenly they were right in among the cows.

"Look there, Doc!" Lee said in an urgent whisper, pointing to a large cow grazing calmly not ten feet from them.

"That's Betty," she noted.

Betty was a bit swaybacked and had a very long, swishing tail.

"Now watch," Lee Ayers said.

She called out in a loud voice: "Get on, Betty!"

The cow tensed, and jerked her head up. Her eyes showed terror. She urinated. She began to walk in a bizarre, stiff-legged gait, like a crippled toy soldier. Then she stopped, urinated again, and finally went back to grazing peacefully.

"Well?" Lee Ayers demanded.

Didi didn't respond. She had never seen anything quite like it.

"Watch this," Lee said. She picked up a small pebble and flung it lightly at Betty. It hit the animal's flank.

Once again the cow went through her strange ritual, repeating the steps in exactly the same order.

"Look," Didi said, "let's get Betty into the barn, and I'll examine her. We'll also start a workup —blood, urine, stool."

Lee Ayers produced a lead rope, and she and the doctor started walking slowly toward Betty.

"Hold up!" Charlie called out suddenly. He hadn't moved at all.

Didi turned to him impatiently. "What?"

"It's the Grass Staggers, Doc."

Didi was startled by the sureness of his diagnosis.

"No, Charlie. That's a beef cattle thing."

"Dairy cows get it too! I seen it before! At least twice in the late seventies."

Lee Ayers jumped in. "What is he talking about?"

Didi elucidated.

"Grass Staggers is the farmers' name for hypomagnesemic tetany. It's a metabolic disorder. The low levels of magnesium and high levels of potassium in certain grazing pastures combine to limit magnesium absorption. In other words, we're talking about a major deficiency."

Didi paused. The wisdom of Charlie's diagnosis became apparent. These "organic" cows ingested only pasture—no commercial feed at all.

"Is it bad?"

"From what I know of the disorder, Mrs. Ayers, Betty is in no danger . . . *now.* But the later stages get nasty. Convulsions and death."

"Can't you do anything?"

"Oh yes. It's treated quickly and easily. An IV injection of calcium and magnesium, along with a sedative."

"Maybe you ought to do the whole herd," Lee suggested.

"Yes," Didi agreed. "I think that—"

Her cell phone began to ring like a chirping bird. Didi pulled the phone out of the side pocket of her carpenter's jeans and answered the call.

It was Trent Tucker, one of her "elves." Like Charlie Gravis, Mrs. Tunney, and Abigail, Trent had come with the house and property after Didi's mother died. The daughter could not in good conscience kick out the mother's charity cases, so they remained, working for room and board. Trent was essentially the handyman, a diffident, difficult kid of twenty-four who could never find real work.

"I'm calling from the old quarry," he said.

"What are you doing up there?"

"Look, this sounds crazy, but I just saw Huck."

"You mean Rose's Huck?" Didi asked incredulously.

"Yeah. The corgi. He just trotted out of the woods, skinny and all beat up. Saw me and ran back in."

She didn't know what to say. When her best friend in Hillsbrook, Rose Vigdor, had suddenly packed up and left without telling anyone or leaving a forwarding address, she had of course taken her three dogs with her. The two German shepherds, Aretha and Bozo, and the corgi, Huck. No one had seen hide nor hair of Rose and her entourage since then. No one had heard from her.

"Did you hear what I said?" Trent asked.

"I heard."

Dr. Nightingale tried to think clearly. What were the possibilities? Only two. Trent had just seen a stray corgi. Since it wasn't a common breed in the Hillsbrook area, he assumed it was Huck. Or Rose was visiting the area secretly. But why? Why wouldn't she look Didi up? Why wouldn't she explain why she had left so suddenly and without a word?

Didi turned to Lee Ayers. "I'll be back late this afternoon with the IV preparations. About four o'clock. Just have them all in the barn by three."

Dr. Nightingale and her assistant climbed into the red Jeep and drove five miles to the old stone quarry that had for many years functioned as the town dump. It was closed down in the mid-eighties and filled in with gravel. The quarry was located in the ugliest and poorest section of Hillsbrook, the Ridge, a series of small hills dotted with cabins and derelict trailers. It was rural poverty at its worst: no electricity, no phones, no plumbing. The main industry of the Ridge was stolen vehicle parts.

Trent Tucker was waiting for them, standing alongside his battered pickup truck on the dirt road that led to the quarry. It was the road that the dump trucks used to use—sloping precipitously toward the cusp of the quarry.

"Huck came out of the woods over there. Then he saw me and ran back in."

"Okay. Let's spread out and cover the area," Didi said.

They distanced themselves about twenty feet from one another and entered the woods. It was difficult going, wading through the thick low-lying shrubs and the stunted pin oak and jack pines. The air was dense. Mosquitos hovered in clusters, wood beetles scrambled over their feet, and horseflies buzzed about their ears.

"Here, Huck! Here, Huck!" they kept calling.

They had penetrated about a hundred yards from the road when they heard the growl—a low, spitting, ugly sound.

Then they saw him. Oh yes, Didi thought, that is surely Huck.

The dog was sitting on his haunches, snarling. The clearing in which he sat was sandy.

"He's so damn mangy he looks like a squirrel," Charlie noted. They stopped about ten feet from him. Didi crouched down and held out her hand.

"Here, boy. Come over here. Come on."

The small dog kept his place and kept growling.

Then Didi looked past him and saw what seemed to be a wild flower growing right out of the sandy soil. Trent saw it also. He broke a limb off a stunted oak, sprinted past the dog, and began to scrape away at the sandy earth.

Huck charged him and fastened his teeth on the digger's boot. Trent ignored the dog.

As he scraped, the wild flower emerged in its full shape. One didn't need a field manual to identify it. It was a lock of Rose's hair.

The ground was so porous and the grave so shallow, it took only moments to realize what was being excavated—three partially decomposed bodies. Rose Vigdor and the two German shepherds.

Only the silver dog tags and the blond hair had maintained their form and color.

The little dog grew weak in his assault on Trent's boot. He lay down and stared at Dr. Nightingale. She could not meet his gaze.